AMERICAN DRAGONS

AMERICAN DRAGONS

Twenty-Five Asian American Voices

Edited by Laurence Yep

HarperTrophy®

A Division of HarperCollinsPublishers

Longhang Nguyen: "Rain Music" by Longhang Nguyen. Copyright © 1993 by Longhang Nguyen

Judith Nihei: "Koden" by Judith Nihei. Copyright © 1993 by Judith Nihei

Lane Nishikawa: "They Was Close, Those Brothers" from *Life in the Fast Lane*. Copyright © 1982 by Lane Nishikawa. Reprinted by permission of the author.

Ann Tashi Slater: "There's No Reason to Get Romantic" by Ann Tashi Slater. Copyright © 1993 by Ann Tashi Slater

William F. Wu: "Black Powder" by William F. Wu. Copyright © 1993 by William F. Wu

Julie Yabu: "A Lesson from the Heart" by Julie Yabu. Copyright © 1993 by Julie Yabu

Wakako Yamauchi: "And the Soul Shall Dance" by Wakako Yamauchi. Copyright © 1974 by Wakako Yamauchi. Reprinted by permission of the author.

Steve Chan-no Yoon: "Stoplight" by Steve Chan-no Yoon. Copyright © 1993 by Steve Chan-no Yoon

American Dragons
Twenty-Five Asian American Voices
Copyright © 1993 by Laurence Yep
All rights reserved. No part of this book may be used or reproduced in any manner whatsoever without written permission except in the case of brief quotations embodied in critical articles and reviews. Printed in the United States of America. For information address HarperCollins Children's Books, a division of HarperCollins Publishers, 10 East 53rd Street, New York, NY 10022.

Library of Congress Cataloging-in-Publication Data
American Dragons : twenty-five Asian American voices / edited by Laurence Yep.
    p.   cm.
Includes bibliographical references.
    Summary: Includes short stories, poems, and excerpts from plays that relate what it is like growing up Asian American.
    ISBN 0-06-021494-5. — ISBN 0-06-021495-3 (lib. bdg.)
    ISBN 0-06-440603-2 (pbk.)
    1. Asian Americans—Literary collections. 2. Children's literature. [1. Asian Americans—Literary collections. 2. Literature—Collections.] I. Yep, Laurence.
PZ5.A51144   1993   92-28489
810.9'9282—dc20   CIP
                                                                      AC

Typography by Al Cetta
❖
First Harper Trophy edition, 1995

To Alvin Dea,
who's had great ideas ever since the first grade

CONTENTS

PREFACE

There is a dragon in each of us. It waits within consciousness like a dragon sleeping beneath the surface of a pool. A whispered prayer, a cry, a breeze can rouse it from the depths. The dragon comes in dreams; it comes in the waking day.

In ancient times dragons lured poets into the sky and carried them to faraway places. In China the devout symbolically tried to rouse dragons from the pools. If there is one animal that is synonymous with Asian mythology and art—and the heart—it is the dragon.

When Asians came to America, they brought these inner dragons with them; and these dragons left their tracks as they wandered into what Virginia Hamilton calls "The Great American Hopescape"—that vast psychological wilderness created by the American Dream.

This is not the place to do a survey of Asian American history except to say that it is not monolithic—just as there were differences between the German and Russian Jews who emigrated here.

Different Asian groups came at different times. Sometimes one group replaced the other as in migrant labor. However, the purpose was always the same: so their families could survive.

Asian Americans come not only from China and Japan but from the many countries around the Pacific Rim, including the Philippines, Korea, India and even

Tibet. Recently there have been new waves of immigrants, especially from Southeast Asia, countries such as Vietnam, Thailand, Cambodia and Laos. A comprehensive survey of Asian American literature and cultures would require several volumes. I have instead tried to follow six trails into different regions of that Hopescape. The writers in this anthology represent just a portion of the diversity of theme and talent among Asian American writers. They trace those six paths with strength and clarity and wit.

—Laurence Yep

AMERICAN
DRAGONS

Identity

A dragon appears in many guises and is always adaptable, the survivor par excellence. Asian Americans display the same versatility as they move back and forth between their Asian culture and their American one. As Philip Slater states in *The Pursuit of Loneliness*, on the one hand, America stresses competition, individualism, independence and technology. An Asian culture, on the other hand, stresses cooperation, community, interdependence and tradition. The cultures pull in opposite directions, and it is the soul of the Asian American that provides the rope for that tug of war.

Who am I? What am I? These are questions my students raised most often when I taught creative writing in Asian American Studies at UC, Berkeley and UC, Santa Barbara. Wing Tek Lum speaks eloquently about that limbo in his "Translations."

Sometimes the search for an identity transforms the American Hopescape into a war zone. Whatever their culture, almost all Asian American writers are veterans of the battlefield represented by Darrell Lum's Chinese school. In his "Yahk Fahn, Auntie," Darrell Lum chronicles the guerilla warfare that takes place not only in that classroom but at the dinner table as well.

Steve Yoon's "Stoplight" poignantly describes the dilemma of being caught between the trenches in a no-man's land.

The dance floor is another spot where cultures can war with one another. "Miss Butterfly" is the ironic title that Toshio Mori gives to the dilemma of Asian American women who are caught in the crossfire between American and Asian American male stereotypes.

Asian American parents burden their children with a heavy load of expectations before they send them into the Hopescape; but like medieval European knights these children can become so weighed down with armor and weapons that they can barely move. In her "Hollywood and the Pits," Cherylene Lee shows that dropping that burden is the first step toward a ceasefire. Perhaps the next steps are what Lensey Namioka suggests in the excerpt from her novel *Who's Hu?*: Find what you want to do and what you are good at.

WING TEK LUM is a prize-winning Chinese American poet who resides in Hawaii.

TRANSLATIONS

for Jeffery Paul Chan in appreciation for his letter
to the editor, *New York Review of Books*, April 28, 1977

1
Ghosts: they conjure
up childhood
scenes—me running around in
old bedsheets, reading
about Casper
next to a comic
rack, marvelling at
the trick camerawork for Cosmo G. Topper.

Gwái: I am older now,
sometimes catch previews
to those Shaw Brothers horror
films, at the
library research ancient
rites of exorcism for
the baneful
who brought pestilence and
drought. There are also,
I have
learned, Old Demons who wear

white skin
and make believe
they behave
like men.

2

The Chinaman gave
the Demon what
the former thought
the latter thought
were things
Chinese: a comedy
of errors,
part fawning, part
deception and contempt.
There is no word for
fortune cookie in Cantonese.

3

Tòhng Yàhn Gāai was what
we once called
where we
lived: "China-People-
Street." Later, we mimicked
Demon talk
and wrote down only
Wàh Fauh—"China-Town."
The difference
is obvious: the people
disappeared.

DARRELL LUM *is a Chinese American from Hawaii who writes fiction and plays in both pidgin and standard English. With the help of a grant from the Rockefeller Foundation, he recently completed a new play. "Yahk fahn" means eat rice in one of the Chinese dialects.*

YAHK FAHN, AUNTIE

Jimmy would sit at the table with his fork and his father would spoon out the rice. Jimmy always got the plate with the chip in it and was always served last. That meant he got the bottom of the pot where the rice was brown and clumpy and soggy sometimes if it wasn't cooked long enough. Jimmy once asked how come he was always last. His father would look up from his spooning and say, "Because you're the littlest. When you're not the littlest then you won't get served last." Jimmy said, "Oh," and thought about that for awhile. It wasn't until later when he was sitting around and thinking about things that he figured out that he would always be the littlest because everybody was bigger than he. Or at least it would be a long time before he wasn't the littlest. His father probably hadn't thought of that but that was okay. Besides now that he was big enough to use a glass cup instead of his old chewed up plastic one and sometimes pour his own milk he didn't really mind being last for the rice.

Once Jimmy asked Auntie Tsu when he would be an uncle. Aunt Tsu laughed at first but explained that when she got married and had children then she would let Jimmy be an honorary uncle. He asked her right the next day if she were married yet but Auntie Tsu was busy and just said, "No," and looked away. Jimmy was confused for a long time about Auntie because his mother had said that she wasn't really his aunt. He asked his mother how come and she said Auntie came from China, that she ran away with grandmother and came to live with them when po-po died. But when Jimmy asked why, his mother was busy.

Once in awhile they would go to eat at a restaurant and Jimmy would be sure to announce, "I not going sit at the high chair."

"Okay, okay. What do you want to eat," his father would ask. Jimmy would always answer, "Chow mein kind," because they came in plates not bowls.

"Yum cha, Jimmy," Auntie Tsu would urge.

"I want Coca-Cola, I no like tea."

"Jimmy, the tea is very good," Auntie would persist.

"Don't force him if he doesn't want to," his mother would say. "But no Coke. You already had one before lunch."

Jimmy would pout and stab his fork at his noodles but secretly triumph over Auntie Tsu. She can have her lousy tea he would think and busy himself with his fork making such a racket that sometimes the other people in the restaurant would look and his father would quietly say, "One more sound out of you and that fork Jimmy . . ." His father would never finish his sentences when he spoke to Jimmy like that. Jimmy would always imagine horrible things and he would always stop.

He stood watching them crank the coffin down. They said Auntie was asking for him just before she died. She had died before he had gotten a chance to see her. He must've been in L.A. changing planes. Jimmy stood in line and watched the rest of the family toss a clump of dirt into the hole and poke a stick of wispy incense into the burner. He followed their actions feeling clumsy and conspicuous.

The feast for Auntie Tsu was arranged before the gravestone; chicken, eggs, and pork, five bowls of rice and a cup of tea beside each one. He imagined one bowl was for Auntie and the rest was for the family. Jimmy watched an uncle tip each bowl and toss a bit of food on the ground. When he was through the scene looked as if Auntie had nibbled at the chicken and had a bite of rice. Auntie must be smiling Jimmy thought because his mother could never make chicken as well as Auntie could. Jimmy wondered which bowl was his. He thought he saw one of them with a tiny chip but he wasn't sure.

It was a good funeral with wailers and flutes and lots of relatives and crying. But Jimmy was tired and wished he understood the chants and the bells and the burning paper. A Caucasian man tried to take pictures but some uncle threatened him and chased him away. Jimmy clutched a piece of candy and a lee-see, a quarter wrapped in red paper which someone said was "From your Auntie to sweeten the sorrow."

There was a party after the funeral where one uncle stripped to his undershirt and solemnly urged everyone to eat. Jimmy sat down and when the food came, everyone ate. There was no fork at the table. Jimmy meant to ask the waitress but by then everyone at the table had noticed that he wasn't eating.

"I'm not very hungry, excuse me." He made for the door but another unknown relative intercepted him and handed him a bowl and a pair of chopsticks. "You're supposed to keep these and the armband," he told Jimmy.

Jimmy walked back to the car in the wake of his father's explanation to the group, "He's had a long trip back."

Why had he come back. Seven years. He hadn't come back for seven years. He watched his hands drop the bowl, the chopsticks following, and he wished he understood why.

"Jimmy, yahk fahn lo!" Auntie Tsu would call. Jimmy would usually refuse to answer and pretend not to hear. He knew perfectly well that it meant to come and eat but he always waited for Auntie to come downstairs and mutter, "Lo-lo," and tell him to hurry and get inside before dinner got cold. She always said that even when they had cold ginger chicken.

"Use your chopsticks, Jimmy," Auntie would say. She would pick a particularly juicy piece of chicken and reach across the table and plunk it down on top of his rice.

"No, I no like."

"I don't want to, Jimmy," his mother would correct gently. Jimmy would take his plate and put his mouth to the edge and shovel the food into his mouth with a fork. He liked when everyone ate from plates. But when Auntie Tsu cooked, they used bowls and drank tea. Jimmy would always get angry when Auntie would forget his favorite chipped plate and only leave chopsticks and a bowl at his place. Jimmy would get his plate from the top shelf and push the tea away all the while crying silently with little hiccups. Auntie would say she was sorry she forgot and pick something good from the table and deposit it in Jimmy's plate. Jimmy would keep on pouting until he was sure everybody at the table knew how he felt about the matter and then eat Auntie's morsel.

His mother and father and Auntie would always talk Chinese when there was something they didn't want Jimmy to hear. Sometimes when Jimmy asked what they said his father would say, "If you did a little studying for Chinese school you'd know."

"Huh!" Jimmy would say. "All we ever do is write the same old stuff and say the same old stuff and read the same old stuff." Sometimes though, when Auntie Tsu said something that sounded interesting, Jimmy would say it to himself over and over so he wouldn't forget and listen for it in Chinese school. He never asked anybody because he was afraid it might be something bad or dirty and he didn't want anyone to think his Auntie Tsu said bad things. Because of this, he never found out what they meant because the teachers at school never talked about the same things as Auntie Tsu.

9

Jimmy never learned much in Chinese school because he always wrote things in American. He did his homework by writing the first strokes of each character down the page, then the second, and the third instead of completing each character one at a time. His assembly line characters were always poorly spaced but he was always the first to finish.

It was windy the next day when Jimmy walked through Chinatown, his nose curling at the suddenly familiar sounds and smells. The wind blew steadily until the old men sitting on crates in the storefronts had to fold their newspapers and go inside. The wind smelled of salted things, fish, cabbage, and duck from the corner grocery where his mother used to poke around the bins to choose a salted fish worthy of being cleaned and soaked and steamed. The old storefront was just as he remembered it, plastered with "Kent with the Micronite Filter" posters and the torn green awnings that were lowered each afternoon to keep the sun out of the dark smelly interior.

Jimmy turned the corner and walked into a restaurant. The greasy menu was written in two languages and Jimmy held it trying to remember the words. The waitress brought a glass of water, slapped a pair of chopsticks down on a napkin and stood with pad in hand waiting for his order.

"Uh . . . one order of chow mein, uh . . . gee yuk chow mein?" Jimmy ordered.

"Yut gwo order gee yuk chow mein," she repeated.

He mixed some soy sauce and hot mustard in a little

dish and listened as his order was relayed to the kitchen, "Gee yuk chow mein." The response through the swinging doors was a lazy "Wai," accompanied by a splattering of oil.

The steaming noodles were delivered to his table about five minutes later and were deposited along with the check on the table's edge. The tiny mountain of noodles topped with pork, broccoli, and gravy fogged his glasses as he bent over the plate. He fumbled with the chopsticks for awhile managing to catapult a few pieces of meat into his mouth before he gave up. He flagged the waitress down, asked for a fork and absently complained that his teacup was badly cracked and chipped. She brought him a fork and went away.

When Auntie Tsu would take him to the temple, Jimmy would have to kneel and pray before the gilt Buddha. He bowed three times and made the praying motions until his aunt, satisfied as to his reverence, would give him a coin wrapped in red paper. He would have to wait until Auntie finished lighting the incense and stick the bunch into the sand-filled holder before she allowed him to go across the street to spend his lee-see. Auntie Tsu stayed in the temple to talk to the round-faced monk with the shaven head. The monk always smiled, a wan, kindly smile and sometimes would teach Auntie a new chant. Jimmy thought that his aunt could chant the best of all the ladies there. He didn't understand what everything meant but then again he never asked. He was afraid that he was supposed to know and that he wouldn't get any more lee-see if he asked.

He left the restaurant, wandering through the street rediscovering the wrinkled men and dirty children who played in the leaning balconies of the tenement houses shouting epithets in Chinese. An old woman carrying a worn shopping bag recognized him from the funeral and asked him something in a whining voice. Her eyes were wet and she clung to his shirt tugging at the sleeve. She kept pointing and gesturing and Jimmy kept saying, "Me no talk Chinee, no talk Chinee." He gave her a dollar and fled.

Jimmy watched her sit, carefully sweeping her hands across her rump first then settling down like a hen coming to roost. He watched her eyebrows dance as she talked in a careful Midwestern tone slipping occasionally into a local accent. He said, "Yes, that's right," so that she would continue. She blinked a lot, her eyelids scotch taped into a Caucasian double fold. Haole. Chinese eyes trying to be haole . . . Caucasian eyes. Jimmy looked around and every table had the same haole-ed oriental. Ironed flat straight hair and carefully made up noses to make it look as if there really were a bridge. He ordered another scotch. She had a mai tai. She giggled and lowered her eyes and crossed and recrossed her legs, her nylons swishing. He was supposed to take her hand now and suggest they go somewhere but he didn't feel like it. He knew the signals. He had learned them in the Army. Only there it had been Chicano chicks and a few Puerto

12

Ricans. But they all looked about the same and always crossed their legs when the time came. Instead he ordered dinner.

They waited. Jimmy's dinner came in several bowls of painted porcelain and a large wooden tub of rice; hers came on a single platter, steak and potato. The waitress offered Jimmy a fork but he waved her off and gamely struggled with his chopsticks while she loitered over her meal quizzing him on New York and the fashions. He scooped out more rice. It had been a long time since he had rice. Or at least rice that stuck together and could be spooned in clumps. Haole rice always had butter in it and fell into the plate in a loose pile. He served himself then looked up to see her watching. Without asking, he scooped some rice over her baked potato.

Auntie Tsu would have laughed because she had once written to ask whether he had met a nice Chinese girl in New York. And here he was back home with a nice Chinese girl and a baked potato.

"Yahk fahn, Auntie," Jimmy said softly.

STEVE CHAN-NO YOON *is a Korean American whose fertile mind takes its inspiration from southern California, where he resides.*

STOPLIGHT

It's times like these that I wish I could be someone else. I mean, I love myself and all, and I wouldn't normally change a thing, but for right now, I just wish I could be some other person in some other place. I mean, I just can't imagine any kid my age feeling at ease with his parents, in an Italian restaurant, on a Saturday night.

"Are you ready to order?" says the waiter as he slithers over to our table. He is wearing black slacks and a white button-down shirt, and his head shines in the light from the pound of hair gel that he uses to slick back his hair.

I lean back in my chair, and I tap my fingers on the table, and I slowly look up at him. "No. We're still waiting for someone," I say, and with that the waiter walks away.

"When the Kims get here, I want you to be nice," my mom says as she looks at her deeply tanned face in the mirror of her compact. "They are coming all the way out here from South Pasadena, so be nice." She snaps her compact shut and levels a stare straight up at me.

Looking back at her cold dark eyes, and at that thin line of a mouth, I say with a sigh, "Fine."

The restaurant is as slick and glossy as the pages from a magazine. The walls are done up in a nice soft pastel color, and covering some of the larger spaces on those walls are paintings that depict wealth and sex in bright Day-Glo colors. There are spotlights brighter than daylight shining down on all the tabletops. The tables themselves are too high and the chairs are uncomfortable, but they look nice, and I guess that is all that matters in a place like this. The only thing that I like about the whole setup is a pair of red and green neon lights that circle the room. They blink on and off, and they hum softly to themselves when the restaurant lies silent.

The tables of the restaurant are full of the rich white tan Americans who litter the streets of Los Angeles. Young white couples known as yuppies sit in their chairs sipping foreign light beers. One man sits at his table talking on a cellular phone while his wife flirts with the help. I can hear one couple, behind me, talking about how much money they have and about what they can do to make some more. Everybody in the restaurant has an almost dazed look about them, as if they had just finished selling off what little remained of their souls. They all look spent.

We are the only Asians in the whole restaurant, and this reminds me of a piano we once owned. All the keys were black or white except for one, and that key was stained a dull yellow. It looked more like plastic than ivory. I swear, it makes you feel kind of cheap and dirty in a weird sort of way.

"So, son, how is everything?" my father asks me,

speaking in his native Korean language.

"Everything is fine," I answer, using my native English.

"Do you like your new school?" he asks me as he puts out his cigarette.

"Yeah, it's great. Why did we have to leave this time?"

His gaze drifts around the room, and with no emotion in his voice he says, "We left because of you."

"But I wanted to stay."

Ignoring what I just said, he looks down at his watch and lights another cigarette. You see, our family is one of those moving families. We move for whatever reason there is, and so far we've lived in almost every city in America. It's given me a good sense of what this country is all about, but what is that really worth?

It would be nice to call a place home for more than a few months. I sometimes wonder, when we are flying or driving to our newest home, what a normal life would be like. I wonder what it would be like to live in a three-bedroom house, with a two-car garage, and a dog barking in the backyard. I also wonder what it would be like to live with white skin, with white parents in this white world. It must be strange, that's for sure.

"Weren't they supposed to be here at nine?" my father asks my mom.

"There must be a lot of traffic. You know, they are coming all the way from South Pasadena. That's a long drive," my mom says as she twirls her diamond ring around her finger.

"Do you need anything?" my dad asks me.

"No. I'm fine," I answer. They do this to me every time we go out. They try and make up for a week's worth of neglect in one night by asking me if I need any money. I wish I could tell them that money isn't my problem, but I just can't.

"When are they getting here?" my father asks again.

But at that exact moment the Kims come into the restaurant. Mr. Kim is a short stout man of about fifty years. He looks like one of those average Asian men who work about twelve hours a day, seven days a week, for about thirty some odd years, until the stress gives them a heart attack. He's the type of guy who sacrifices his entire existence for the sake of his family, but what do you get off on, Mr. Kim? What is your drug?

Mrs. Kim is a darkly tanned woman in her late forties. You can just tell that like my mom this woman loves the game of golf and a good session of gossip. Her specialties are a good back swing and an open flowing mouth.

The two men sit down at once, greeting each other with Buddha-like smiles. The women sit and smile affectionately at each other and start their usual talk. They talk about other people and other people's children, and about how so and so just got into Harvard, while so-and-so just got out of jail. In this community so long as you get good grades, you can murder someone and still be considered an angel. The stupid children are the bad ones, and the smart children are the saints. That's a fair way of doing things, isn't it?

When the waiter sees that our table is complete, he comes over. I look down at the menu, and I order for both my parents and myself. It's easier this way. I mean, my dad can order like no one else in any Oriental restaurant, but in a place like this it's almost embarrassing.

"How do you like Los Angeles, Austin?" Mrs. Kim asks me.

"It's different."

"You'll get used to it," she says with a big smile.

They leave me alone after that, which is fine with me. I just sit there eating, watching, and thinking, and before I know it, the dinner is over. My father and Mr. Kim argue over the bill for a few minutes, battling to see who will pay. To them it is an honor to pay and a disgrace not to. My father eventually grabs the check rudely out of the hands of Mr. Kim, and he pays the bill.

We walk out of the restaurant with mints rolling in our mouths. We stand there in the crisp night air waiting for our cars to be delivered. The sky above is clear, cleaned by the rains that fell earlier that day.

The streets are wet and the air still smells damp.

We get into our car and start on our way home. We are the only ones on the road, which is something that doesn't really happen that often in L.A. Usually these streets would be filled with mile upon mile of screaming cars, like a lava flow from some erupting auto plant. But tonight, the only actions in the intersection we are coming to is a lone newspaper drifting in the wind like a sagebrush in an old western ghost town. There is only one thing for me to look at, and this is the red stoplight.

I look up at the stoplight, and I try to figure out what it means. I know that the red light means stop and that the green light means go, but I cannot figure out what the blinking yellow light stands for. What does being yellow mean? The best answer that I can come up with is an in-between: go if you want to but stop if you don't. I hate being in between things, I really do, but it all doesn't matter because the light that is on is red, and all that it tells me is stop.

"Oh, look isn't that Mr. Lee at the side of the road?" my mom says as she looks through her side window.

I break the daze that I am in and look over to the side of the road. I have not noticed it before, but over to the side of the road sits a car with a flat, and around that car sits a family much like ours, but with a daughter and not a son. I look over closer at the girl sitting alone on the sidewalk staring down at the ground.

She has black straight hair flowing about her face in a way that only nature could have put it. Her face is oval shaped and covered in pearl-white skin. Her mouth is full and red, and her nose is pert, yet not conceited. Her eyes are large and brown, like those of a deer, and the only thought that is in my mind at this time is that she is a person I have to know.

"Hey, who's Mr. Lee?" I ask.

"It's one of your dad's employees," my mom says with a turn of her head.

"Why don't we help?" I say from the backseat.

"We should," my father says as he pulls over to the side of the street. He gets out of our car and goes over to his employee, and I go straight over to the girl sitting on the sidewalk.

"Hi. How's it going?" I say as I walk over toward her.

"Who are you?" she demands of me.

"My name's Austin. Our fathers know each other, and we pulled over to help," I say.

"Well, go ahead and help," she says, using her hand to point limply at the tire.

"You don't have to take that attitude about it," I say as I slowly walk away.

"Wait, I'm sorry. My name's Julie, and you just didn't pick the right time to try and talk to me. I'm a little annoyed right now," she says as she turns her head toward the tire.

"Well, do you think that maybe if I got your number and called you later, you would be in a better mood to talk?"

"Sure," she says with a smile, and she has a real nice smile. "That wouldn't be too bad."

Boldness with the females isn't usually my game, but sometimes it comes when the times call for it. All the way home I repeat her name and her number in my head as if it were a poem that will open up to some secret meanings. Julie, and Julie, I think in my mind.

The next day I call her on the phone. We try and talk, but nothing comes out right. It's hard to have a conversation on the phone with someone you hardly know; so we decide to go out and talk in person. We both agree that a standard dinner-movie date won't do the job. Instead we plan a simple conversation over some coffee. We pick a nice little café on Pacific Coast Highway to be our meeting place. "We" is the new word for me, and I must admit that "we" sounds better than "I."

The air of the café is full of the smoke that billows from the few people who are smoking. The smell of freshly ground coffee beans penetrates the air like the smell of burning leaves on a windy October day. The smells, strangely enough, go well with the brown wooden furniture and the green plants that hang from the ceiling.

Mixed in with the constant whir of the coffee grinders and the espresso machines, the soft murmurs of people talking fill the sound waves of the room. The corner that I sit down in is right in front of a huge bay window that frames the beach scene outside. Sea gulls float in the sky like kites in a strong wind. The waves tumble under a bright-red sun that looks as if it is ready to crash down into the sea. I sit there in my seat waiting for Julie to come, and I am not even sure if she will show, but I don't worry about it too much. I just sit there, and I stare out the window.

I sit there for what seems like forever, until Julie finally walks in through the door. She is wearing a light sundress that clings to her body, leaving little room for the imagination but room enough. I can't help but think about how perfect she looks, and how much of a dream she is.

"Did you wait long?" she asks me.

"No, not that long."

"You know, I barely got out of the house today," Julie says as she sits down at the table. "My mom was making all these excuses for me not to go out. She finally told me that I shouldn't go out with a guy like you who has a bad reputation. Can you believe that?"

"I'm used to that. Trust me," I say as I take a sip of my

coffee. "But that's just the thoughts of the older generation who overexaggerate things anyways. I mean, I don't think that just because I've made a few mistakes, I should be considered the devil reincarnated. Do you?"

She shakes her head, saying no. "Sometimes it's just so hard to understand our parents, isn't it?" she says as she plays with her coffee mug on the table. "We've got this huge generation gap to deal with, and on top of that we've got a cultural gap too. It really makes a conversation impossible sometimes."

"So it's just not me? Thank god—I thought I was going crazy there for a second." I say this and we both laugh for a second. "My mom tells me that you got into a pretty decent college."

"I just got accepted to Princeton."

"Really! Congratulations," I say.

"Thanks," she says with a soft humble smile.

"What are you going to study there?"

"I'm going to be a psychology major. I want to eventually study dreams."

"Wow, that's different. What do your parents think of this?"

She takes a sip of coffee and licks her liquid mustache with her tongue. "Well, of course they want me to become an accountant or something boring like that, but I've got to do what's going to make me happy, and not them. Right?" She says this in a way that makes me feel that she is in need of some reassurance.

"You know what I think?" I say while leaning forward as if to tell her a secret. "I think that they gave up their dreams and decided to live life in a stable way, and now they're miserable for it. So they feel jealous and resentful toward us for going for our dreams. That's why they discourage us."

"I guess that could be true. I honestly don't think that my parents have any dreams besides the ones that are connected to me," she says with a certain sadness in her eyes.

"God, for the longest time my parents wanted me to become an engineer, and take over the family business, but there's no way in hell I would ever do a thing like that," I say with determination in my voice.

"Then what do you want to do?" she asks as she puts her elbows on the table, and she rests her face in her hands.

"Me?" I say with a smile, and then whisper, "I was put on this earth to give my parents hell."

Julie looks at me, and she tilts her head back as her mouth opens wide. She laughs—and not one of those geisha-girl giggles, either, but a real hearty laugh. "God, you are so weird," she says as she still laughs.

In an Asian society that is full of conforming mannequins who all dress the same, look the same, and act the same, it is always nice to be noticed. Most of the time being different or weird is the only way that some of us can have an identity that isn't generic.

"Thank you," I say smiling. "You're pretty weird yourself."

"A good weird, right?" she says with a smile.

"Right."

We continue our talk about all the things we hate, and about all the things we love. We talk about all of the common things that we've shared, but basically we talk about how much we understand each other. To be understood, in this world that doesn't understand me, is one of the greatest things that I can ever feel. I mean, isn't that what we are all looking for, a little acceptance?

Sitting there in our own little world, I close my eyes and I wish to myself for this night to never end, but it does. The sun finally melts into the sea, and a blue darkness covers the sky. We both inhale the cool salty sea air as we walk outside toward the beach. There is a set of benches along the boardwalk that we sit down on.

"This is one thing that you don't get much of in New York," I say as I point out to the sea.

"Why did you move out here?"

"Do you want the truth or what my parents want me to tell you?"

She pauses for a second and then says, "The truth."

"Well, there was this Korean guy who owned a deli on our block. He was a J.O.J.—you know, just off the jet— and he spoke only a few words of English. He was from the old school, closed minded and a bit racist," I say, taking a breath to catch my thoughts. "One night a bunch of my friends and I went into the store and started messing with the deli man. I translated the things that he said, and the situation got out of hand. A fight broke out, but the deli man made it sound like we were robbing the store. He pressed charges on everyone but me."

"Why didn't he press charges on you?"

"Because my dad went in to talk to him. But after that there was a big demonstration because one of my friends was black. We moved because it got really uncomfortable for us to live there anymore."

"So you went in there to prove to your friends that you were on their side, but it all backfired," she says.

"All I wanted to do was to prove to everyone that just because we looked alike, it didn't mean that we thought alike," I say, looking down.

We sit there in silence for a few moments, and then we walk over to the parking lot where both our cars sit. There is a fluorescent streetlamp that flickers a yellow light across our faces. She walks up to her car and turns to me.

"I had a good time," she says. "Call me tomorrow."

"Sure," I say, walking closer. I look at her and move my head forward to kiss her.

Kisses can be childish or even meaningless at times. There is, however, a feeling one gets when two pairs of lips press up against each other that is neither childish or meaningless. It is as if this moment were meant to be.

Actually we never kissed. Hell, I don't even know if Julie is her name. I don't even know if a girl like Julie does exist. I once read a book, though, that said that the subconscious does not distinguish between reality and fantasy. So in that sense she is real to me, and maybe someday I will meet a girl like Julie. Then maybe I won't have to feel like an alien, alone on a strange planet. The stoplight turns green. Our car moves forward, and this jars me out of my thoughts. We drive on home and the stoplight keeps changing.

Born in 1910 in Oakland, California, TOSHIO MORI *was
a prolific Japanese American writer whose writing was cut
short only by his death in 1980.*

MISS BUTTERFLY

The doorbell rang and Sachi ran nimbly to the door.
"Yuki!" she called to her younger sister. "I think they're
here!"

"I'll be out in a moment," Yuki answered from the bedroom.

Sachi opened the door and found an old man standing
on the porch. "Oh hello, Hamada-*san*," she said, her face
plainly revealing disappointment.

"Good evening, Sachi-*chan*," greeted Hamada-*san*, en-
tering the hall. "Is your father home?"

Sachi looked up and down the street and then closed
the door. "Yes. Hamada-*san*. He's in the living room. Go
right in."

The old man looked admiringly at her, pausing for a
word with her. "My, you are growing prettier every day. Is
Yuki-*chan* home too?"

She smiled and nodded. "We're going to the dance
tonight with our boy friends," she added eagerly.

Hamada-*san*'s face fell but brightened quickly. "Do you
still have those Japanese records—the festival music, I
mean?"

"Yes," Sachi replied, looking puzzled. "We still have them."

"And is your phonograph in good condition?" he asked.

She nodded impatiently, anxious to return to her dressing.

"Good!" cried the old man, clapping his hand. "Please come into the living room. I wish to have a talk with you and your father."

"But I will be late for the dance!" she protested. "I must dress now."

Hamada-*san* looked pleadingly at her. "Please, Sachi-*chan*. Please, this is my special request."

The old man led her into the living room where her father sat reading the Japanese daily. "Saiki-*san*, how are you?"

Saiki-*san* dropped his paper and took off his glasses. "Good evening, Hamada-*san*. Anything new?"

Hamada-*san* dropped into the easy chair, leaning forward eagerly. "Saiki-*san*, I have one special request to make of your daughters tonight. It will bring me much happiness, and I shall forget that I am a lonely man for a short while. Please ask Sachi-*chan* and Yuki-*chan* to do it for an old man's sake."

"What is it you want?" asked Saiki-*san*.

"You may recall my repeated request in the past. I want to see the cherry blossom, the *taiko* bridge, and hear the Japanese paper houses hum when the wind blows. I want to dream of the pine-studded hills, the crystal-clear lakes, Fujiyama, Miyajima, and New Year festivals . . . the old Japan. My mouth waters with the flavors of the island fruits, rice cakes, and fish. My heart runs away with the color of the kimonos, the plaintive songs, and the loss of my many ancestors. Do you get it?"

Sachi groaned and waved her hands protestingly.

"So you wish them to perform Japanese folk dances," Saiki-san said, smilingly.

Hamada-san beamed and eagerly added, "Odori—that's what I mean. Please, Sachi-chan, wear your beautiful kimono tonight and perform one dance for me. Just one, that is all I ask. I want to capture my lost memories and dream. Dance for an old man and let him enter his old world for several minutes."

"No, I won't," she said emphatically, standing impatiently by the door. "I won't."

"Daughter, what are you saying?" Saiki-san said. "Make Hamada-san happy tonight. Wear your kimono and dance."

"One dance, Sachi-chan," begged the old man, humbly bowing. "For your father's old friend. He is poor and cannot reward you. Otherwise, he would shower you with gifts."

"I don't want anything," said Sachi, and looking at her father added, "I hate to wear kimono."

Hamada-san looked horrified. "Ah, Sachi-chan!" he cried. "Please do not say that. Don't you Nisei girls realize the truth? When you wear your bright, colorful kimono you are the most beautiful women in the world. Your eyes brighten up, your figure becomes symmetrical, your gestures move naturally. Don't you see, Sachi-chan?"

Sachi stood speechless, hesitating whether to laugh or smile.

"Sachi, why don't you like to wear kimono?" her father asked.

"It takes so much time, and I feel clumsy and stiff," she replied.

Hamada-*san* smiled and shook his head. "You don't look it when you wear it. You are merely saving that for an excuse. I don't believe it."

She looked at her watch and cried, "I've lost five minutes already."

"What time does the dance begin?" Saiki-*san* asked her.

"At eight sharp," Sachi answered eagerly. "Papa, may I go now?"

"Saiki-*san*! Please remember your old-time friend," cried Hamada-*san*.

From the bedroom came the younger sister in her glittering white evening gown. "I heard what you said about Nisei girls, Hamada-*san*," Yuki said, smiling. "Sachi, let's do one *odori* for him. It won't take but ten minutes, dressing and all, and it'll make him happy. I have your gown and the rest of your things out, all ready for you to slip them on."

Sachi thought for a moment. "All right. I'll do it," she said suddenly. "Papa, please select the record and be ready when we come out."

"I'll do that," Hamada-*san* said, beaming. "Saiki-*san*, just sit and relax."

Eagerly he began sorting out the record albums. The

girls rushed into the bedroom. After much deliberation the old man selected two records and went to the phonograph.

"This is my favorite," Hamada-*san* said to his friend, holding up one record. "This is about a day in autumn in Japan. The wind blows and the leaves fall. The sky is clear and the air is beginning to cool. The chants of the insects are dying out and late harvest is about over. The flowers shrivel and the last of the leaves flaunt their brilliant colors in the wind, and the day awaits the icy blast of winter."

The girls' father sat silently, lit his pipe, and blew smoke. He watched his old friend poring over the words of another record and wished he had some kind of an answer for him.

"It's a beautiful piece," Hamada-*san* informed, indicating the first record. "Especially when dancers perform skillfully as Sachi-*chan* and Yuki-*chan*."

The two girls hurriedly skipped into the room. They wore their best kimono, a colorful design on silk, enhancing their youthful beauty.

"Are you ready with the music, Hamada-*san*?" asked Yuki. "We're all set."

At the sight of the girls in kimono Hamada-*san* sat up, his eyes wide with open admiration. "Beautiful, beautiful! The whole world should see you now."

Sachi laughed it off, and Yuki smiled happily. They went over to the phonograph and inspected the record. Satisfied with the selection they rushed Hamada-*san* to a seat.

"Sit down and enjoy yourself," Sachi said. "We'll watch the record. Hamada-*san*, there will be positively one performance tonight."

"Two?" the old man asked timidly.

"Positively one," Sachi repeated.

The music began, and the girls waited alertly for their cue. Hamada-*san* poked Saiki-*san* in the ribs as the two girls performed. He clapped his hands, keeping time with the music. His eyes, round with excitement, twinkled. His body swayed this way and that way. Then he forgot his friend, the time and place. Long after the music stopped and the girls paused by the phonograph, Hamada-*san* sat fixedly.

"Good night, Hamada-*san*," called the girls at the door.

"Wait!" cried Hamada-*san* springing to his feet. "Sachi-*chan*, Yuki-*chan*, one more! The parasol dance! Please, just one more. Please!"

The girls looked at each other, hesitating. Hamada-*san* ran to the phonograph and started the record going. "Hurry, girls. Get your parasols!" he cried.

The high notes of a *samisen* and the mixed instruments cut the air. The girls ran to get their parasols. Hamada-*san* beamed and clapped his hands in tune with the music. Saiki-*san* sat comfortably in his chair, his eyes closed, and sucked his pipe.

The girls returned and instantly snapped into the dance. Their parasols opened and twirling, they leaped over imaginary puddles and worried about their slippers. They looked up at the sky, their hands out to see if the rain was falling. Their faces bright with smiles they twirled their parasols with happy abandonment. The sun is out once again, and they forget the puddles, the mud, and discomfort. Their bodies, minds, and hearts join to greet the sunny day, their somber aliveness increasing to gay abandon.

Once more Hamada-*san* sat motionlessly, unheeding the end of the music and the dance. Sachi stopped the phonograph.

"Wonderful! Wonderful!" cried Hamada-*san*, becoming alive. "I shall never forget this performance."

"Yuki, how much time have we?" asked Sachi hurriedly.

"Exactly ten minutes," Yuki said. "Let's hurry."

The girls dashed into their room.

"Wasn't it wonderful, Saiki-*san*? Wasn't it?" asked Hamada-*san*.

"Yes, they were pretty good," replied Saiki-*san*.

When the girls returned to the room their father was reading the paper. Hamada-*san* sat silently by himself in the corner, his eyes staring in the distance.

"How do we look, Papa?" Sachi asked, the two girls showing off their new evening gowns.

"Swell," Saiki-*san* said, looking up.

"What do you think of them, Hamada-*san*?" Yuki asked old man. "Hamada-*san*!"

"Please don't ask me such a question, Yuki-*chan*. Not tonight," Hamada-*san* said sadly.

Sachi looked puzzled. "What's happened to you, Hamada-*san*? Are you ill?"

"Nothing is the matter with me. I'm all right," he said, cheering up with an effort. Then he added, "Sachi-*chan* and Yuki-*chan*, please be careful with your kimono. Don't let the moths get into them."

"We'll be very careful with them," Sachi promised.

"And don't you forget the *odori*. Keep brushing up."

The girls nodded obediently. Outside a horn blared.

"Oh, they're here!" cried Sachi, running to the window.

"Isn't it exciting?" Yuki cried, moving to her sister's side. "We're going to have a good band tonight."

The girls waved their hands, and the horn tooted again. "Good night, Hamada-*san*. Good night, Papa," they said.

"What is this dance? What kind?" the old man asked his friend, watching the girls skip out of the house.

"A social dance. Popular American pastime," answered Saiki-*san*, without looking up from his paper.

In the living room Saiki-*san* smoked incessantly and the place became stuffy. He continued to read the paper. Hamada-*san* sat mutely in the corner, his eyes smarting with smoke. He could have gone outside for a bit of fresh air but did not move. His eyes took in the phonograph, the record albums, the spots where the girls danced, and the room that was now empty. In the silence he heard the clock in the hall ticking.

—1939

CHERYLENE LEE is a multitalented Chinese American who writes not only stories but also plays and poetry.

HOLLYWOOD AND THE PITS

In 1968 when I was fifteen, the pit opened its secret to me. I breathed, ate, slept, dreamed about the La Brea Tar Pits. I spent summer days working the archaeological dig and in dreams saw the bones glistening, the broken pelvises, the skulls, the vertebrae looped like a woman's pearls hanging on an invisible cord. I welcomed those dreams. I wanted to know where the next skeleton was, identify it, record its position, discover whether it was whole or not. I wanted to know where to dig in the coarse, black, gooey sand. I lost myself there and found something else.

My mother thought something was wrong with me. Was it good for a teenager to be fascinated by death? Especially animal death in the Pleistocene? Was it normal to be so obsessed by a sticky brown hole in the ground in the center of Los Angeles? I don't know if it was normal or not, but it seemed perfectly logical to me. After all, I grew up in Hollywood, a place where dreams and nightmares can often take the same shape. What else would a child actor do?

"Thank you very much, dear. We'll be letting you know."

I knew what that meant. It meant I would never hear from them again. I didn't get the job. I heard that phrase a lot that year.

I walked out of the plush office, leaving behind the casting director, producer, director, writer, and whoever else came to listen to my reading for a semiregular role on a family sit-com. The carpet made no sound when I opened and shut the door.

I passed the other girls waiting in the reception room, each poring over her script. The mothers were waiting in a separate room, chattering about their daughters' latest commercials, interviews, callbacks, jobs. It sounded like every Oriental kid in Hollywood was working except me.

My mother used to have a lot to say in those waiting rooms. Ever since I was three, when I started at the Meglin Kiddie Dance Studio, I was dubbed "The Chinese Shirley Temple"—always the one to be picked at auditions and interviews, always the one to get the speaking lines, always called "the one-shot kid," because I could do my scenes in one take—even tight close-ups. My mother would only talk about me behind my back because she didn't want me to hear her brag, but I knew that she was proud. In a way I was proud too, though I never dared admit it. I didn't want to be called a show-off. But I didn't exactly know what I did to be proud of either. I only knew that at fifteen I was now being passed over at all these interviews when before I would be chosen.

My mother looked at my face hopefully when I came into the room. I gave her a quick shake of the head. She looked bewildered. I felt bad for my mother then. How could I explain it to her? I didn't understand it myself.

We left saying polite good-byes to all the other mothers.

We didn't say anything until the studio parking lot, where we had to search for our old blue Chevy among rows and rows of parked cars baking in the Hollywood heat.

"How did it go? Did you read clearly? Did you tell them you're available?"

"I don't think they care if I'm available or not, Ma."

"Didn't you read well? Did you remember to look up so they could see your eyes? Did they ask you if you could play the piano? Did you tell them you could learn?"

The barrage of questions stopped when we finally spotted our car. I didn't answer her. My mother asked about the piano because I lost out in an audition once to a Chinese girl who already knew how to play.

My mother took off the towel that shielded the steering wheel from the heat. "You're getting to be such a big girl," she said, starting the car in neutral. "But don't worry, there's always next time. You have what it takes. That's special." She put the car into forward and we drove through a parking lot that had an endless number of identical cars all facing the same direction. We drove back home in silence.

In the La Brea Tar Pits many of the excavated bones belong to juvenile mammals. Thousands of years ago thirsty young animals in the area were drawn to watering holes, not knowing they were traps. Those inviting pools had false bottoms made of sticky tar, which immobilized its victims and preserved their bones when they died. Innocence trapped by ignorance. The tar pits record that well.

I suppose a lot of my getting into show business in the first place was a matter of luck—being in the right place at the right time. My sister, seven years older than me, was a member of the Meglin Kiddie Dance Studio long before I started lessons. Once during the annual recital held at the Shrine Auditorium, she was spotted by a Hollywood agent who handled only Oriental performers. The agent sent my sister out for a role in the CBS *Playhouse 90* television show *The Family Nobody Wanted*. The producer said she was too tall for the part. But true to my mother's training of always having a positive reply, my sister said to the producer, "But I have a younger sister . . ." which started my show-biz career at the tender age of three.

My sister and I were lucky. We enjoyed singing and dancing, we were natural hams, and our parents never discouraged us. In fact they were our biggest fans. My mother chauffeured us to all our dance lessons, lessons we begged to take. She drove us to interviews, took us to studios, went on location with us, drilled us on our lines, made sure we kept up our schoolwork and didn't sass back the tutors hired by studios to teach us for three hours a day. She never complained about being a stage mother. She said that we made her proud.

My father must have felt pride too, because he paid for a choreographer to put together our sister act: "The World Famous Lee Sisters," fifteen minutes of song and dance, real vaudeville stuff. We joked about that a lot,

"Yeah, the Lee Sisters—Ug-Lee and Home-Lee," but we definitely had a good time. So did our parents. Our father especially liked our getting booked into Las Vegas at the New Frontier Hotel on the Strip. He liked to gamble there, though he said the craps tables in that hotel were "cold," not like the casinos in downtown Las Vegas, where all the "hot" action took place.

In Las Vegas our sister act was part of a show called "Oriental Holiday." The show was about a Hollywood producer going to the Far East, finding undiscovered talent, and bringing it back to the U.S. We did two shows a night in the main showroom, one at eight and one at twelve, and on weekends a third show at two in the morning. It ran the entire summer often to standing-room-only audiences—a thousand people a show.

Our sister act worked because of the age and height difference. My sister then was fourteen and nearly five foot two; I was seven and very small for my age—people thought we were cute. We had song-and-dance routines to old tunes like "Ma He's Making Eyes at Me," "Together," and "I'm Following You," and my father hired a writer to adapt the lyrics to "I Enjoy Being a Girl," which came out "We Enjoy Being Chinese." We also told corny jokes, but the Las Vegas audience seemed to enjoy it. Here we were, two kids, staying up late and jumping around, and getting paid besides. To me the applause sometimes sounded like static, sometimes like distant waves. It always amazed me when people applauded. The owner of the hotel liked us so much, he invited us back to perform in shows for three summers in a row. That was before I grew too tall and the sister act didn't seem so cute anymore.

Many of the skeletons in the tar pits are found incomplete—particularly the skeletons of the young, which have only soft cartilage connecting the bones. In life the soft tissue allows for growth, but in death it dissolves quickly. Thus the skeletons of young animals are more apt to be scattered, especially the vertebrae protecting the spinal cord. In the tar pits, the central ends of many vertebrae are found unconnected to any skeleton. Such bone fragments are shaped like valentines, disks that are slightly lobed—heart-shaped shields that have lost their connection to what they were meant to protect.

I never felt my mother pushed me to do something I didn't want to do. But I always knew if something I did pleased her. She was generous with her praise, and I was sensitive when she withheld it. I didn't like to disappoint her.

I took to performing easily, and since I had started out so young, making movies or doing shows didn't feel like anything special. It was a part of my childhood—like going to the dentist one morning or going to school the next. I didn't wonder if I wanted a particular role or wanted to be in a show or how I would feel if I didn't get in. Until I was fifteen, it never occurred to me that one day I wouldn't get parts or that I might not "have what it takes."

When I was younger, I got a lot of roles because I was so small for my age. When I was nine years old, I could pass for five or six. I was really short. I was always teased about it when I was in elementary school, but I didn't mind because my height got me movie jobs. I could read and memorize lines that actual five-year-olds couldn't. My mother told people she made me sleep in a drawer so I wouldn't grow any bigger.

But when I turned fifteen, it was as if my body, which hadn't grown for so many years, suddenly made up for lost time. I grew five inches in seven months. My mother was amazed. Even I couldn't get used to it. I kept knocking into things, my clothes didn't fit right, I felt awkward and clumsy when I moved. Dumb things that I had gotten away with, like paying children's prices at the movies instead of junior admission, I couldn't do anymore. I wasn't a shrimp or a small fry any longer. I was suddenly normal.

Before that summer my mother had always claimed she wanted me to be normal. She didn't want me to become spoiled by the attention I received when I was working at the studios. I still had chores to do at home, went to public school when I wasn't working, was punished severely when I behaved badly. She didn't want me to feel I was different just because I was in the movies. When I was eight, I was interviewed by a reporter who wanted to know if I thought I had a big head.

"Sure," I said.

"No you don't," my mother interrupted, which was really unusual, because she generally never said anything. She wanted me to speak for myself.

I didn't understand the question. My sister had always made fun of my head. She said my body was too tiny for the weight—I looked like a walking Tootsie Pop. I thought the reporter was making the same observation.

"She better not get that way," my mother said fiercely. "She's not any different from anyone else. She's just lucky and small for her age."

The reporter turned to my mother, "Some parents push their children to act. The kids feel like they're used."

"I don't do that—I'm not that way," my mother told the reporter.

But when she was sitting silently in all those waiting rooms while I was being turned down for one job after another, I could almost feel her wanting to shout, "Use her. Use her. What is wrong with her? Doesn't she have it anymore?" I didn't know what I had had that I didn't seem to have anymore. My mother had told the reporter that I was like everyone else. But when my life was like everyone else's, why was she disappointed?

The churning action of the La Brea Tar Pits makes interpreting the record of past events extremely difficult. The usual order of deposition—the oldest on the bottom, the youngest on the top—loses all meaning when some of the oldest fossils can be brought to the surface by the movement of natural gas. One must look for an undisturbed spot, a place untouched by the action of underground springs or natural gas or human interference. Complete skeletons become important, because they indicate areas of least disturbance. But such spots of calm are rare. Whole blocks of the tar pit can become displaced, making false sequences of the past, skewing the interpretation for what is the true order of nature.

That year before my sixteenth birthday, my mother seemed to spend a lot of time looking through my old scrapbooks, staring at all the eight-by-ten glossies of the shows that I had done. In the summer we visited with my grandmother often, since I wasn't working and had lots of free time. I would go out to the garden to read or sunbathe, but I could hear my mother and grandmother talking.

"She was so cute back then. She worked with Gene Kelly when she was five years old. She was so smart for her age. I don't know what's wrong with her."

"She's fifteen."

"She's too young to be an ingenue and too old to be cute. The studios forget so quickly. By the time she's old enough to play an ingenue, they won't remember her."

"Does she have to work in the movies? Hand me the scissors."

My grandmother was making false eyelashes using the hair from her hairbrush. When she was young she had incredible hair. I saw an old photograph of her when it flowed beyond her waist like a cascading black waterfall. At seventy, her hair was still black as night, which made her few strands of silver look like shooting stars. But her hair had thinned greatly with age. It sometimes fell out in clumps. She wore it brushed back in a bun with a hairpiece for added fullness. My grandmother had always been proud of her hair, but once she started making false eyelashes from it, she wasn't proud of the way it looked anymore. She said she was proud of it now because it made her useful.

It was painstaking work—tying knots into strands of hair, then tying them together to form feathery little crescents. Her glamorous false eyelashes were much sought after. Theatrical make-up artists waited months for her work. But my grandmother said what she liked was that she was doing something, making a contribution, and besides it didn't cost her anything. No overhead. "Till I go bald," she often joked.

She tried to teach me her art that summer, but for some reason strands of my hair wouldn't stay tied in knots.

"Too springy," my grandmother said. "Your hair is still too young." And because I was frustrated then, frustrated with everything about my life, she added, "You have to wait until your hair falls out, like mine. Something to look forward to, eh?" She had laughed and patted my hand.

My mother was going on and on about my lack of work, what might be wrong, that something she couldn't quite put her finger on. I heard my grandmother reply, but I didn't catch it all: "Movies are just make-believe, not real life. Like what I make with my hair that falls out—false. False eyelashes. Not meant to last."

The remains in the La Brea Tar Pits are mostly of carnivorous animals. Very few herbivores are found—the ratio is five to one, a perversion of the natural food chain. The ratio is easy to explain. Thousands of years ago a thirsty animal sought a drink from the pools of water only to find itself trapped by the bottom, gooey with subterranean oil. A shriek of agony from the trapped victim drew flesh-eating predators, which were then trapped themselves by the very same ooze which provided the bait. The cycle repeated itself countless times. The number of victims grew, lured by the image of easy food, the deception of an easy kill. The animals piled on top of one another. For over ten thousand years the promise of the place drew animals of all sorts, mostly predators and scavengers—dire wolves, panthers, coyotes, vultures—all hungry for their chance. Most were sucked down against their will in those watering holes destined to be called the La Brea Tar Pits in a place to be named the City of Angels, home of Hollywood movie stars.

I spent a lot of time by myself that summer, wondering what it was that I didn't have anymore. Could I get it back? How could I if I didn't know what it was?

That's when I discovered the La Brea Tar Pits. Hidden behind the County Art Museum on trendy Wilshire Boulevard, I found a job that didn't require me to be small or cute for my age. I didn't have to audition. No one said, "Thank you very much, we'll call you." Or if they did, they meant it. I volunteered my time one afternoon, and my fascination stuck—like tar on the bones of a saber-toothed tiger.

My mother didn't understand what had changed me. I didn't understand it myself. But I liked going to the La Brea Tar Pits. It meant I could get really messy and I was doing it with a purpose. I didn't feel awkward there. I could wear old stained pants. I could wear T-shirts with holes in them. I could wear disgustingly filthy sneakers and it was all perfectly justified. It wasn't a costume for a role in a film or a part in TV sit-com. My mother didn't mind my dressing like that when she knew I was off to the pits. That was okay so long as I didn't track tar back into the house. I started going to the pits every day, and my mother wondered why. She couldn't believe I would rather be groveling in tar than going on auditions or interviews.

While my mother wasn't proud of the La Brea Tar Pits (she didn't know or care what a fossil was), she didn't discourage me either. She drove me there, the same way she used to drive me to the studios.

"Wouldn't you rather be doing a show in Las Vegas than scrambling around in a pit?" she asked.

"I'm not in a show in Las Vegas, Ma. The Lee Sisters are retired." My older sister had married and was starting a family of her own.

"But if you could choose between . . ."

"There isn't a choice."

"You really like this tar-pit stuff, or are you just waiting until you can get real work in the movies?"

I didn't answer.

My mother sighed. "You could do it if you wanted, if you really wanted. You still have what it takes."

I didn't know about that. But then, I couldn't explain what drew me to the tar pits either. Maybe it was the bones, finding out what they were, which animal they belonged to, imagining how they got there, how they fell into the trap. I wondered about that a lot.

At the La Brea Tar Pits, everything dug out of the pit is saved—including the sticky sand that covered the bones through the ages. Each bucket of sand is washed, sieved, and examined for pollen grains, insect remains, any evidence of past life. Even the grain size is recorded—the percentage of silt to sand to gravel that reveals the history of deposition, erosion, and disturbance. No single fossil, no one observation, is significant enough to tell the entire story. All the evidence must be weighed before a semblance of truth emerges.

The tar pits had its lessons. I was learning I had to work slowly, become observant, to concentrate. I learned about time in a way that I would never experience—not in hours, days, and months, but in thousands and thousands of years. I imagined what the past must have been like, envisioned Los Angeles as a sweeping basin, perhaps slightly colder and more humid, a time before people and studios arrived. The tar pits recorded a warming trend; the kinds of animals found there reflected the changing climate. The ones unadapted disappeared. No trace of their kind was found in the area. The ones adapted to warmer weather left a record of bones in the pit. Amid that collection of ancient skeletons, surrounded by evidence of death, I was finding a secret preserved over thousands and thousands of years. There was something cruel about natural selection and the survival of the fittest. Even those successful individuals that "had what it took" for adaptation still wound up in the pits.

I never found out if I had what it took, not the way my mother meant. But I did adapt to the truth: I wasn't a Chinese Shirley Temple any longer, cute and short for my age. I had grown up. Maybe not on a Hollywood movie set, but in the La Brea Tar Pits.

LENSEY NAMIOKA *is a Chinese American who is well known for her historical and fantasy stories. She writes about not only her own heritage but also her husband's Japanese culture. The following is an excerpt from her entertaining novel* Who's Hu?

WHO'S HU?

I was tired of being a freak.

My father was a professor of mathematics at M.I.T., and whenever I got 100 on my math test (which was pretty often) my high school teachers would say, "I know where Emma Hu gets help with her homework . . . cackle . . . cackle. . . ." The rest of the class usually cackled along. At first I didn't see why they were so nasty about it. Later I discovered that girls in this country weren't supposed to be good in math. The teachers didn't like it when Arthur Aldrich—our self-styled math genius—corrected their mistakes in class. They hated it a lot more when I did.

In China there was nothing wrong with girls being good at math. In fact, Chinese women were supposed to keep the household or business accounts. But in America, when I opened my big mouth to correct my algebra teacher—in broken English, yet—everyone thought I was a freak. Once I thought I would cheat on my math test by deliberately making a couple of mistakes, but when it came to the point, I just couldn't do it. Mathematics was too beautiful to mess up.

On most days I wasn't too bothered by my math grades, but lately I had begun to worry. I was a senior at Evesham High, a high school in the suburbs of Boston, and the senior prom was only three weeks away. Who was going to ask a Chinese girl math whiz? According to my friend Katey, everybody went to the prom except the freaks.

Katey was blonde, pretty, and tall. She had been booked for the prom since her junior year, ever since she began going steady with her current boy friend. I was just over five feet, and when we walked to our classes together, we looked like Mutt and Jeff.

She was even more anxious than I was to see me at the prom. At lunchtime she kept pressing me. "Emma, all the rest of us are going, and it won't be fun if you're not there!"

There were murmurs of agreement from the rest of our set at the lunch table. I sat silent, too choked to speak. These were genuine friends, and they were sorry at the thought that I might be left out. I couldn't allow myself to be classified with the freaks and the weirdos who never went to anything.

After lunch the first class I attended was math. Just being in the classroom made me feel better. I liked to look around the room at the portion of the blackboard painted with a permanent white grid for graphing equations, the hanging cardboard models of regular polyhedra we had made as a class project, and the oak shelf containing plaster models of conic sections and various surfaces. My favorite was the hyperbolic paraboloid, or saddle, with its straight lines neatly incised in the plaster.

The class was Advanced Mathematics, intended for seniors who were going into science or math and who had already taken algebra, geometry, and trig. The course covered analytic geometry, calculus, and a little probability theory. Actually, it wasn't so much the content of the course that I liked best: it was the teacher, Mr. Antonelli. He was a short man only a little taller than I, and he had a swarthy face dominated by a huge beak of a nose. Unlike my other math teachers (one of them even a woman), he didn't seem to find it bizarre that a girl should do well in his class. As for my being Chinese, I doubt if he even noticed. Mr. Antonelli didn't care if you were a Martian eunuch, as long as you did the math correctly.

Today Mr. Antonelli gave the impression of suppressed excitement. He clearly had something on his mind, because for the first time I remember, he let one of the boys do a maximum-minimum problem without checking the second derivative to see if it was an inflection point. Arthur Aldrich and I beat each other to a draw in pointing out the mistake. Mr. Antonelli acknowledged our reproof almost absentmindedly. He certainly was preoccupied.

With five minutes left of the period, Mr. Antonelli made an announcement: "Class, you remember that last fall you all took the semi-final exam for the Sterns Mathematics Prize. Today I received word of the results."

The Sterns was a mathematics prize given annually to a high school senior in Massachusetts. The award was for $200, but the prestige it carried was immeasurable. Never in the history of the Sterns Prize had it been won by a girl.

"Now," Mr. Antonelli went on, "it is an honor for our school if a student here makes it to the finals. Well, we've got not just one student, but two who are going into the finals. One is Arthur Aldrich."

Arthur was a tall, gangly boy with hair so blond that it looked almost white. With his long nose and sharp chin, he reminded me of a white fox in one of the Chinese fairy tales. Arthur had very few stumbling blocks in his life. His family was comfortably off, he did well in every subject in school, and he was a credit to the Evesham High School track team. In spite of his successes, Arthur was too arrogant to be popular.

"The other," Mr. Antonelli announced, "is Emma Hu."

The class cheered. My thoughts were in a whirl. I thought I had fallen down badly on the exam the previous fall because there were two problems I hadn't been able to do. Now it seemed that my performance hadn't been so bad after all.

I have only the vaguest memories of my other classes that afternoon. I barely realized when the final bell rang. Leaving school, I almost hugged my books to my chest. It was like waking up on my birthday and finding a pile of presents outside my door.

My mother probably felt like this when she looked

over a new piece of music, and my father when he received a new set of Chinese pulp novels.

I was so absorbed that I didn't hear footsteps coming up behind me. I jumped when Arthur's voice spoke in my ear. "I want to talk to you."

"About what?" I asked, surprised. To my knowledge he had never asked any girl to anything before. In Arthur's ranking of animal intelligence, girls came somewhere between sheep and myna birds. Of course that made me even more of a freak in his eyes.

Arthur and I must have made a strange-looking pair. His ash-blond hair curled around his thin foxy face, while my long hair, blue-black and straight as a linear function, framed my heart-shaped face. Not only did we belong to different races, we hardly belonged to the same species. The only thing we had in common was mathematics.

When he had seen that I threatened to become a rival, Arthur began a systematic campaign to discourage me. In this he had the support of our previous math teachers. They kept hinting that for a girl to do well in math was unfeminine, unnatural, and unattractive.

At first I hadn't been too bothered. My English had been shaky, and subtle hints were lost on me. Anyway, being teased about my math had been submerged in the larger misery of being an alien. But by my junior year at Evesham, I began to be really uncomfortable. In my trig class I made a lot of mistakes in looking up trigonometric functions, and my math grades slid. My parents were disturbed but couldn't think of a reason. It was my older brother, Emerson, who had looked over my homework papers and found my mistakes. He insisted on having my eyes checked, and when I turned out to have 20-20 vision, he gave me a stern lecture and told me to shape up. My grades went back up.

In our Advanced Mathematics class, Arthur had found no support from the teacher, Mr. Antonelli. Although Mr. Antonelli was a wonderful teacher, his manner was dry and impersonal. He kept personalities out of the classroom entirely.

By using our last names, he made me forget I was the only girl in a class with eight boys. He also made all of us feel very adult.

Arthur grinned now. In the illustrations of my Chinese fairy tale book, foxes grinned with their mouths forming a big V. Arthur's smile was just like that. "I hear you want to go to the senior prom but can't find anyone to take you. I have a simple proposition to make: I'll take you to the prom—refreshments, corsage, dinner afterward, the whole works—if you'll drop out of the Sterns exam."

The sheer gall of his proposition took my breath away, and for a moment I was too astounded even to be angry. In the end my main reaction turned out to be triumph. "So you're really afraid I might do better than you on the exam!" I said, unable to hide my satisfaction.

Two spots of color appeared on Arthur's pale cheeks, but he kept his foxy grin. "I can do better than you any day, don't you worry! But I know you're desperate to go to the prom. Every red-blooded, normal high school senior goes to the prom, right?"

I said nothing. The price of being a red-blooded,

normal high school senior was pretty high.

"Well?" demanded Arthur.

I was determined to be equally curt. "No," I said.

At that, Arthur's normally deep voice went up. "What do you mean, no? You've decided to give up the prom?"

"Arthur, if I accepted your offer just to be able to go to the prom, I'd always be ashamed of myself."

There were some sputters as Arthur finally convinced himself I really meant what I said. "This is your last chance, Emma. Nobody else in the whole school would dream of asking you."

"There are more important things than the prom, Arthur."

"Now you're sounding high and mighty, aren't you?" Arthur sneered. "Don't give me that, Emma. Everybody in school knows you're dying to go."

"It's true, I was dying to go to the prom," I said wearily. "But I've changed my mind."

Arthur's voice went up farther and became almost shrill. "Why does a girl want to take the Sterns exam anyway? Do you want to be known as a freak all your life?"

I swallowed. "Not everybody thinks I'm a freak just because I like mathematics."

"You want to bet? What do you think your friend Katey will say when she hears you turned down your last chance to go to the prom? You're a drag on her already, and this will really be the last straw!"

That hurt. To be rejected by Katey's circle and to go back to my isolation again—the thought was unbearable.

But to accept Arthur's shabby offer was worse, much worse.

"There is no point in talking about this anymore, Arthur," I said.

He stormed away without another word.

"I'm terribly sorry. I couldn't help overhearing."

I turned around and saw it was Kim. He was a Korean boy who was one of my mother's music students.

It was almost a relief not to have to pretend. "It doesn't matter," I said. To my fury, my lips were beginning to quiver. "There isn't a person in school who doesn't already know I haven't been able to find a date for the prom. It's been a joke for so long that I don't even feel humiliated about it anymore."

But that was a lie.

Kim looked as if he were trying not to laugh. "I don't even try to understand all these American customs anymore. But this prom sounds like some sort of native ritual or tribal dance."

He was a foreigner in America and not bothered by it at all. He was even inviting me to join him in enjoying the amusing antics of the natives.

"Don't you feel lonely sometimes?" I asked, remembering my loneliness the first day of school on discovering I was to be the only Chinese there. That loneliness I suffered until Katey and her friends took me in.

Kim only smiled and shook his head. "I'm too busy. Schoolwork is hard for me because of my poor English, and after school all my time is taken up with practicing. Even if I had the money, I wouldn't go." He looked at me curiously. "You are devoted to mathematics the way I am to music, aren't you? I think I heard your mother say so."

I nodded, grateful for these words. He considered our situations to be comparable, and he didn't think that a girl being interested in math was any stranger than a boy being interested in music.

Now that Kim's reserve had broken down, we were less awkward in each other's company. As we chatted at the bus stop, I discovered that what I had taken as shyness was actually an unusual degree of self-sufficiency. Kim made little effort to cultivate friends because he didn't need them. Considering that he had been studying piano with my mother for more than a year, I was dense for not having seen this sooner. Of course I had made no attempt to talk to him either. With my lousy ear for music, I had simply regarded Kim as a breed apart. This was my first opportunity to see that he was a teenage boy, and a nice one.

As Kim got on his bus, he said, "You should try to do the best you can on the exam. You owe it to yourself."

When I got home I was still seething over Arthur's humiliating proposal. More than the insolence of his offer, the very idea of dancing with him disgusted me. Yet when I thought of Arthur's foxy grin, I also remembered the faces of the group around the lunch table at school. And I just couldn't bear the thought of being left out of the group, of not belonging.

The next week the kids in school talked about nothing except the prom and what a delirious time they were going to have. I fixed a bright smile on my face and said yes, wasn't it going to be fantastic.

By the end of the week, the effort of maintaining a dreamy look on my face had become a strain, and I was glad to enter the cool, abstract world of mathematics.

One day at the end of the math period Mr. Antonelli called me over. With a suspicious backward glance, Arthur slowly left the room. He probably suspected that Mr. Antonelli might give me some extra coaching.

After Arthur left, Mr. Antonelli turned to me, his smooth, olive face grave. "In the last few days you've been doing indifferent work, Hu. That homework assignment you just got back was a piece of muddled thinking."

I nodded dumbly. He was perfectly right, and I had no excuse to offer.

After a pause Mr. Antonelli said, "Are you getting nervous about the Sterns examination? Is that why you can't concentrate?"

"Oh, no, I'm not nervous about the exam." At least that was no lie. "It's just that . . . well . . . I've had things on my mind lately . . . the senior prom—"

"The prom?" Mr. Antonelli couldn't have looked more startled if I had stood on his desk and done the cancan. "Some of the students devote an inordinate amount of time on school dances, but surely not you?"

He probably meant that as a compliment, but it didn't help my morale. After promising him I'd try to do better, I plodded to my next class. The message was clear: normal girls were interested in dances; Mr. Antonelli had not expected me to be interested in dances; therefore I was not normal. Q.E.D.

After school I didn't join Katey and the others at the bus stop. It was hard work, keeping up all those bubbling remarks about the prom. I just wanted to brood by myself.

Walking away from the others, I heard a step behind me. It was Arthur. "Hey, wait, Emma," he called. "Have you got a minute? Let's go to Horvath's for a soda."

"What is it this time?"

"Come on, don't be so suspicious," Arthur said, grinning. "Can't a boy ask you out for a soda without being accused of ulterior motives?"

Of course he had an ulterior motive, but I did want one of Mr. Horvath's wonderful sodas, and Arthur was buying. So I shrugged and followed him into the drugstore.

Horvath's was a favorite hangout for the kids at Evesham. It was a small place, with a soda fountain and a row of stools on one side of the room and three tiny booths in the back for people wanting privacy. Opposite the fountain was a counter where Mr. Horvath sold everything from swimming caps and roller-skate keys to cheap little aluminum pencil sharpeners that broke the lead of your pencil every time.

Of course I had no choice over the flavor. In his ranking, Arthur said, ice-cream soda flavors were (1) strawberry, (2) vanilla, and (3) chocolate. Personally, I preferred chocolate, but I didn't make an issue of it because the sodas here were good, whatever the flavor. Mr. Horvath made them himself.

I watched him put a scoop of ice cream into a tall conical glass, add strawberry syrup, and then mash the two together, forming a paste. Then he forced a thin stream of soda into the glass, stirring hard until the pink, creamy foam came nearly to the top. Another scoop of ice cream completed the soda. It was lovely. In China we drank a fizzy lemonade, but ice cream was a rare luxury.

When both sodas were made, we carried them to the back and sat down in a booth. Arthur arranged his foxy features into a friendly smile and launched into what sounded like a prepared speech. "You know, you're not a bad-looking girl, Emma. I like the way you wear that cashmere twin set."

I stared at him. This was the first time a boy had ever paid me a compliment. None of the Chinese boys who dated me had ever taken such a liberty, and only someone trembling on the brink of proposing marriage would attempt to make such a personal remark.

To Arthur, my reaction apparently meant that I was overwhelmed by his compliment. He scooped up a spoonful of ice cream and licked it deliberately. "Attraction between an Oriental and a normal American is rare," he continued.

"It's been known to happen," I said dryly.

Arthur was not put off. "What I mean is, I could be really attracted to you, Emma. And I don't get attracted to girls easily. I have high standards." He shrugged modestly. "Not that some of the girls at Evesham High haven't made a play or two. Take Jeanette. She's all right, but she's not exactly a smasher. You know what I mean?"

Arthur was tall and slim, and had ash-blond hair and a thin, narrow face. I suppose you could call him attractive—especially if you were a lady fox. Come to think of it, Jeanette had a narrow foxy face too.

But I kept quiet and merely relieved my feelings with an extra-loud slurp on my straw.

"But look, Emma," Arthur now warmed up to his subject, "your physical appearance isn't so important. I can get used to straight black hair, narrow, slanted eyes and all that. What's hard is getting used to your foreign attitudes."

I began to see his drift now. "Yes? Tell me about my foreign attitudes."

This was the opening Arthur wanted. "Well, it's mostly your attitude toward math. Now, American girls are not all dumb, I grant you that. But their talents are developed in other directions. They can become writers and poets. Some of them go for dancing and acting. I even admit they understand discipline and hard work."

"Magnanimous of you," I murmured.

He didn't hear me. "But science and mathematics, these are not subjects fit for girls, at least not for American girls. You have no idea how it puts a guy off to see a girl studying these subjects. I know you want to stay here and be accepted by American society. But you'll never make it unless you change your attitude."

I had heard enough, and anyway, my soda was finished. "Thank you for the soda, Arthur, and for the compliments," I said, standing up. "It was terribly kind of you to give me such an illuminating lecture on American society in addition."

Two spots of color appeared on Arthur's pale face. "You'll always be an alien unless you change your alien way of thinking."

Arthur's intention was perfectly transparent, I thought,

as I walked to the bus stop. He wanted me to give up on the Sterns exam.

But that didn't mean what he had said was completely wrong. I remembered how it had been with Katey when I was coaching her for the math College Board exam. She wanted to be good enough to get a barely decent score, but she refused to work beyond that, although she had the ability.

Maybe Arthur was right: I was a permanent misfit in America.

On the appointed afternoon, I entered the Boston University classroom where the Sterns examination was being held. The monitor checked my name against his list and nodded. "Good. All fifty of you are now here."

It seemed I was the last one to arrive. For a while I had considered not coming at all. What was the point? I was in no condition to do mathematics. I suppose I came because it would have been too much trouble to tell Mr. Antonelli I was planning to drop out.

We all sat down and arranged our pencils and bluebooks on the desks in front of us. When the monitor passed out the exams, heads bent eagerly over the papers. I looked at the first page with dull despair. There were some diagrams with circles, but nothing made sense to me. In my present state I hardly knew the difference between an ellipse and a circle. An ellipse was just a tired circle.

All around me pencils scratched busily in bluebooks. My pencil was still as I relived my private hell at home. On my left, Arthur glanced up at me. He looked different, and I realized he had applied a pomade on his hair to stick it down. He flashed his foxy grin, and the smugness in it told me I looked a mess. I had not slept at all the night before, and my eyes were red and puffy—not all from sleeplessness.

My watch showed that almost an hour had passed. Already half the time allotted for the exam was gone and I hadn't started a single problem.

I glanced at Arthur again and found his eyes fastened on me eagerly. How many times had he looked this way? He must have noticed that I hadn't done a thing, because when his eyes met mine, his grin widened triumphantly.

I picked up the exam paper and looked at it once more. The writing might as well have been in Greek. Only I could read Greek a little, since I already knew all the Greek letters from seeing them used in mathematics. No, the writing here might as well be in Korean for all I could understand.

Kim entered my mind. He could not afford to give up classical music, for he owed it to himself not to squander his talent.

It was the thought of Kim that finally opened my eyes. I should not try to be something I was not. And I was not, nor could ever be, a normal American teenager. I was going to be a mathematician. This was the Sterns exam, my first opportunity to show my mettle. I could not afford to squander my talent. As Kim had said, I owed it to myself. I had to stop frittering away the precious minutes and get down to work. Having made the decision, I felt a weight lift from my chest.

I glanced down at the examination paper and finally read the problems—really read them. The first problem I might be able to do, but it looked tedious and would probably take too much time. And I didn't have much time left. The second problem—well, maybe I'd skip it and come back to it later. The wording of the third problem was intriguing. I read it over again. At first I thought there was a misprint, because the problem looked impossible—there was simply not enough information given. Because of this, the problem tickled my fancy. I leaned back and thought about it.

Sometimes doing a tough math problem is like playing a game of Pick-up-Sticks. You look at the jumble of sticks and it's a complete mess. But after a while you notice how one stick is supported by a second one, which in turn is supported by a third and a fourth. You begin to see how the various sticks depend on one another. Then it becomes a matter of deciding which stick to take first. Once you manage to take out a few of the key sticks, the rest becomes a cinch.

I looked at the exam problem from several different angles. I considered various equations and saw how they depended on other equations. Suddenly I spotted a key stick. Almost afraid to breathe, I put out my hand and gently wrote down my first equation. This was the first of the key sticks. I breathed easy again. It was a good move. What about a second move? I thought about another equation. But no, that wouldn't do. The whole structure would collapse.

By now I was completely engrossed. My parents, Kim,

Katey all were forgotten. I even forgot Arthur, who was staring at me instead of concentrating on the exam. I considered the jumble of sticks again and I spotted another key stick. Why hadn't I seen it sooner? Gently does it. . . .

And now for the next move. Yes, that was it. And then another deft move. And suddenly there was nothing left of the problem but a few isolated sticks to be picked up—easy pickings.

In the Shadow of Giants

At the center of the Hopescape is a plaza where American culture raises monuments to the ideal American parent. Television, radio, comic books and movies tell children what their parents should be. Ironically, it would be difficult for a parent of any race to measure up to those giant icons.

Furthermore, the many Asian cultures also create their own images of the ideal parent that are not only larger but shaped differently. For instance, there are many Chinese proverbs that warn parents not to spoil a child with praise or that child will become an egomaniac. And one can find echoes of that sentiment in many other Asian cultures. As a result, these Asian American parents will seem indifferent by American standards. However, it would be wrong to think they love their children any less.

If a Chinese American child were to receive high marks in school, the parents might not compliment their child. (This does not mean they do not love the child or are any less proud of their offspring than American parents; but the support they give and the way they express their love and pride takes other forms.)

However, the Chinese American child knows what his or her American peers receive, and so this more traditional set of Chinese American parents may suffer in comparison.

For children, the difference between a parental icon and the reality, can also often create resentment. As they get older, they acquire new yardsticks to use in measuring their parents, and in understanding that their parents have strengths as well as weaknesses.

Growing up as a child on a farm, Janice Mirikitani became all too familiar with her father's flaws. However, her poem "For My Father" shows how a weakness can also be a strength.

As a boy, Alan Chong Lau was chagrined by the bastardization of his Asian culture and his father's broken English. As a man, he came to appreciate the strength and wisdom that underlay his father's words and actions. "a father's wishes" is a poet's record of that journey to that new point of view.

Sometimes, though, the cultural differences can lead to tragic failures—as in a case of sexual abuse. Nicol Juratovac's autobiographical story "Dana's Eyes" describes an Asian parent afraid to deal with an American authority figure.

JANICE MIRIKITANI is a Japanese American poet who lives in San Francisco. Mount Fuji is a Japanese mountain much revered by the Japanese people. Tule Lake refers to the internment camps (see the introduction to the section on World War Two). The incidents with the strawberries happened at their farm in Lodi, California.

Hakujine means Caucasian.

FOR MY FATHER

He came over the ocean
carrying Mt. Fuji
on his back/Tule Lake on his chest
hacked through the brush
of deserts
and made them grow
strawberries

> we stole berries
> from the stem
> we could not afford them
> for breakfast

his eyes held
nothing
as he whipped us
for stealing.

the desert had dried
his soul.

wordless
he sold
the rich,
full berries
to hakujines
whose children
pointed at our eyes

they ate fresh
strawberries
with cream.

Father,
I wanted to scream
at your silence.
Your strength
was a stranger
I could never touch.

iron
in your eyes
to shield
the pain
to shield desert-like wind
from patches
of strawberries
grown
from
tears.

ALAN CHONG LAU *is a Chinese American poet and editor who makes his home in Seattle, Washington.*

a father's wishes—

the birthday letter

"dear son,

wishing you have a very happy birthday this year. you will be 26 years old. the proverb word said—the time and tide wait for no man. i'm sure you know what it means when you got up at such age. it's time to make up the mind what should to do the rest of your life. that's for all human being thinking. hoping you chosen right one to settle down soon. please write as often as you can. i'm still in paradise few more year. i'm getting old and tire and still trying to sell restaurant so we can retire and traveling round the world. hoping the dream come through someday. bye till then.

your love
dad

p. s. thanks your bridge magazine have your poetries published inside. it's very nice. i read all you wrote the poetry."

1

when you have fish
on a platter
soaking in black beans
sublimely scented with spears of green onion
the chinese say
"eat the eye
it's the best part"

a deft jab
pops the pupil out

prong pressure
from tongue's red tip
and the jelly comes squiggling out
of its socket

2

the wok and soup pot
your brass band and funky cooking utensil tympani
symphonics going out
to the american legion
pork chop suey
7th day adventists
water chestnut chow yuk
the doctor   the lawyer   and mother superior
barbecued pork chow mein   pineapple duck
eggflower soup
rotary   lions   kiwanis
crisp fried egg rolls   egg foo young
shrimp chow yuk

the bowling team
coca-cola   grilled special
cut boneless rib steak with
french fries
garbage collector   district attorney
won ton and don't forget
fortune cookie

thirty years later
your act is getting old
cooking out of tune brings on thoughts
of a vacation to honolulu

what can i say to this man
who performs in superduper papercone hat
cosmic white apron
for a full house of mouths
ready to pour sugar in the jasmine tea
melt butter on the steaming rice?

shake your hand?
spray seltzer in baggy eyes
and tell you
there'll be no more rounds
that the gong will not sound again?
superman walks in with donald duck
they both want chicken almond chow mein
and you only got enough for one order
pop, what you gonna do?

father who jabbed out your eyes
and sucked your sockets dry?

"could i have a side order of . . . ?"

"the sign—yes!
can't you read the sign?
CLOSED
PLEASE CALL AGAIN"

3
father
home
to see you

every room familiar
yet half froze as if deserted
in a storm warning
turned into a spider's playground

only the living room is strange
no longer my mother's mess
floor waxed and shining
under a portrait of my sister
is the granite table
with six matching chairs picked up in taiwan
on a group tour

"i see this table
i like it
i have a little money
no use, can't spend nothing
after i dead . . . you know that"
you sit alone
eat at this table with six matching chairs
clip your nails on the sports page

the lights go out
power failure
but you don't stop clipping your nails

4
father
it's hard for me
to talk to you
listen to the sound of my voice
pay no attention
to the words
they are only wagons in the wind
instead hear the creak
of the wheels pleading for oil
it is my young pain
with your old pain
moaning the boatmen's blues
t o g e t h e r

father
you thought you were saving face
even when they cut off your nose
father, let's not say anything
sit at the table
i will serve you the bitter melon
stuffed with fish
i will eat the soft beancurd

notice the way light plays
with bamboo
throwing blades of colour on our skin

so quiet here
only a little noise
this is enough

5

my father
now fifty years bowed
still builds
lean straight planks
of words
to cross
water
he cannot see

when the flood
comes
nothing will remain
but my father
wielding a mop
amidst currents

an old man
sends a card
on a 26th birthday
and writes
"time and tide
wait for no man"

father
is it too late
to say
i love you?

NICOL JURATOVAC is a Korean American who grew up in various parts of San Francisco. She somehow manages to combine law school with her writing.

DANA'S EYES

Cluttered with ripped pages of *Archie* comic books and cardboard boxes, Dana's room resembled a tornado disaster. The sunbeam from her only window picked up the dust that skirted the small room Dana called her castle. "Man! Am I glad to be moving out of this dump," Dana mumbled as though she were speaking to someone in the room, someone who was also watching her wrap her precious crystal unicorn set with colorful *Archie* pages. In four days they would move.

There was something odd about this scene to anyone who knew the imaginative Dana. The "dump" was once her cherished escape from anything that troubled her. It was her hideout. It was her palace. But Dana was now seeing it for what it actually was, the cubicle of a two-bedroom housing project unit. The apartment was home to Dana and her mother. Her sudden distancing from what she had once thought of as her castle was Dana's way of saying good-bye to what she once was a part of and once was.

Though precocious, as her teachers, aunts, and uncles incessantly told her, Dana was also a bit of a realist. This was a problem at times, as it made Dana face things she did not want to face. Her golden hair and hazel-green eyes were deemed by many to be unique, as they clearly contradicted Dana's other, Asian features, primarily her flat eyelids and high cheek bones. Oftentimes Dana thought it much easier to bluntly refer to herself as a "mutt," wanting to avoid further conversation about herself. Physically, this dichotomy of being Irish and Chinese presented a certain beauty in Dana. She was unique-looking, all right. Emotionally, however, Dana was not the quintessential beauty queen, full of flippant frivolous concerns. Instead, she was a roller coaster of feelings. Despite having just turned fourteen, Dana felt as though she were forty years old.

"Dana!" Dana's mother shouted as she walked by her daughter. "You use book pages to wrap?"

Remembering not to always try to correct her mother's broken English, Dana replied, "Calm down, Mom. They're only comic books."

"How much did I pay for those comic books?" her mother asked, her plump figure overshadowing the kneeling Dana. "Those books you always begged me for? I no made of money, you know. Here"—pointing to a stack of Chinese newspapers—"you use these kinds of paper."

"But Mom, I don't need these comic books anymore. I'm getting too old for them. They're just so silly."

Glaring down at Dana with her infamous front-teeth-over-lower-lip look, Dana's mother asked, "You think just because we move out of ghetto you now rich? You think you now can throw away all your things? These things I pay good money for."

Dana's mother always had a way with words, especially when dealing with money. Dana knew this. In fact, Dana knew a lot about her mother. She knew that there were times like this, when her mother acted as though she knew best (as if there were actually some mothers who thought otherwise) and there was no telling her any different. On the other hand, there were moments when Dana felt as though God could not have given her a more loving and devoted mother. After all, it was she who took Dana away from her alcoholic father in a most hostile divorce. It was she who was strong enough to leave her abusive husband with no job and no place to go, and even stronger to bring Dana. And it was she who had gotten Dana the ten-speed Schwinn bicycle on her eleventh birthday and the brand-new Nike tennis shoes before the first day of basketball practice, even if it meant that she had to work two jobs.

Still, there remained a cold, empty separation between mother and daughter. There were times when the ever-so-emotional Dana felt a sense of abandonment from her stoic mother. Of course, Dana knew very well that her mother loved her as much as a mother should love a child. But Dana's mother was different. Dana would frustratedly wonder why her mother would come home from work and sequester herself in her bedroom for what seemed like days. She must be tired, Dana would rationalize. After all, all her friends' mothers who were single worked just as hard and spent little time with their children.

Still, Dana felt very alone as a result of her mother's introverted nature.

"C'mon, my two princesses!" yelled Chuck as he opened the apartment door using the keys that Dana's mother had given him. "It's time to load 'em up." Chuck had just gotten through parking the rented U-Haul truck out on Bay Street. They were moving the bulk of their things today.

Chuck was different from all of Dana's mother's other boyfriends, including Dana's own father. He was not abusive, nor was he ever temperamental about anything. Chuck was a canary bird compared to all the treacherous men in Dana's mother's life. Although Dana never witnessed the beatings by the "monsters," which was how Dana referred to them, the dark-purple bruises on her mother's soft, pale-yellow skin said enough.

Unsurprisingly, Dana missed Chuck awfully when he was not around for more than a day. A longshoreman by trade, Chuck would be gone for weeks at a time, much to Dana's dismay. With his Popeye forearms and his red Uncle Ben beard, Chuck stood at a stubby five feet nine inches and had the most gentle, ice-blue eyes. At thirty-one years of age, he was significantly younger than the forty-five-year-old mother he was dating. Nonetheless, as far as Dana was concerned, he was perfect for her. More important, he was perfect for Dana. Not only had he built the beautiful rosewood desk that comfortably sat in Dana's room, but Chuck took her to see all the Oakland A's games, a favorite event of Dana's. Chuck was also quick and witty. This was complementary to Dana's sarcastic humor that was her trademark. Chuck was a bright addition to Dana's life. He was a friend.

Dana would always remember the day Chuck gave her the unicorn set on her fourteenth birthday. It meant so much to her. Chuck had picked out an entire set of a unicorn family, which included a mother unicorn, a father unicorn, and two little baby unicorns. Dana especially liked the babies. More importantly, Dana thought that the beautiful tinted glass of which the figures were made was uniquely pretty. The glass was a mixture of pink and ruby red, a distinct shade that was juxtaposed with the clearness of a crystal. This family of unicorns represented innocence and innocence lost, the kind of innocence Dana had once had as a child, eating, drinking, and playing with her friends; and the kind of innocence Dana now unwillingly possessed, full of broken promises and broken dreams. The unicorn set gave Dana hope that beauty is possible, that such a harmonious family could, did, and would someday exist.

Everything usually went well with the "family," which now consisted of Chuck, her mother, and herself. That is, until Dana's mother would yell at Chuck to leave. Like all of Dana's mother's male acquaintances, Chuck was not immune to her infamous temper. Although he had broken the three-month mark, the length of time by which most of her men left, Chuck had come close to leaving. During these rough times, it was not as painful for her mother as it was for Dana. Naturally, Dana's mother could get over anything. Besides, Chuck would have been one of many who came in and left by the revolving door of her heart. But to Dana it would have meant losing a substantial part of herself.

"Do we have to hurry so much?" Dana's mother pleaded, applying another layer of lavender eye shadow in front of her bedroom mirror. "I haven't even cooked breakfast yet. We have to eat first, you know." She made sure that she did not apply too much eye shadow number 511. She hated waste. Besides, the Face Place was not to have another sale until a whole month from now.

Answering in his usual spunky manner, Chuck replied, "If my Princess says we must eat, then we shall. What say we hit up Mickey D's for breakfast?"

"No junky food for Dana," Dana's mother warned.

"Mom, it's 'junk' food," Dana corrected.

"I no care. Skin become very bad. I no want Dana to eat McDonald garbage," Dana's mother said with sternness.

"I guess you didn't tell her about their new soy burger Big Macs," Chuck reminded Dana.

"No, I haven't told her yet, but I don't think it's going to make much difference," Dana replied. Then, whispering, she closed in on Chuck's ear. "You know, Chuck, I think she's getting too smart for us. After the fat-free Häagen Dazs scheme, I doubt she'll believe any more of our junk-food justifications."

"Well, just between you and me, kid, if the soy burger Big Macs don't work, then I promise I'll take you to try the biggest and greasiest cheeseburger Wendy's has to offer. Fat free, of course," Chuck whispered with a wink.

"Of course," Dana winked back, nodding her head in her usual facetious manner.

"Why you two always whispering to each other?"

Dana's mother asked while putting on her pink sandals. "Chuck, you act like little boy, and Dana finally acts her own age instead of twenty years older whenever you two together. Oh well, I guess this not so bad for Dana. Dana thinks she too smart sometimes."

As the three got ready to go out for breakfast, Dana dashed back into her room to grab her baseball mitt. There was practice at noon, and she was not going to forget her glove again. The last time she had forgotten, Coach Getty had had the entire team run two laps around Evans Park. Kids do not like running extra laps, especially on account of a girl. It was difficult enough trying to prove herself a worthy member on the all-male team. Dana did not need to create more hurdles for herself.

After eating at Denny's, a "not so greasy" restaurant, according to the ever-so-weight-conscious Dana's mother, the three of them drove past the row of eucalyptus trees that led to Evans Field. Although it was quite early at only ten thirty, for the noon practice, Dana nevertheless wanted to be dropped off at the park. She thought that at least she would be able to help Coach Getty set up the equipment for batting practice, a process that could take hours.

"You guys can drop me off here," Dana said, sitting on the edge of the car seat in her excitement. Chuck pulled into the narrow road that ended at the clubhouse. Dana again made sure that she had her mitt before opening the car door to let herself out. Chuck drove a 1976 Ford station wagon he called "the Beast." One had to be careful so as not to lose anything in the huge backseat area. The inside of the car was so vast that Dana thought it only appropriate that the car was named the Beast. After all, one look at the backseat and one would think that it resembled a huge mouth, ready to suck in any inhabitants. Things could easily get lost back there. Dana especially found the rear seat beneficial, for she had found quarters, dimes, and nickels that had made their way deep between the vinyl.

"Are you sure you don't want us to hang out with you and keep you company?" asked Chuck as he looked around the empty parking lot in front of the clubhouse. Chuck said he thought it a bit unusual, if not eerie, that not one child was playing in the park; not even a voice was heard in the quasi-foggy Saturday morning. "I can hit you some grounders while you wait for practice to start."

"Oh, Chuck," Dana's mother groaned, "she said she'll be fine. Now let's go. We have much work to do back home. All those boxes need to be moved by tonight. Dana," she continued, turning her head toward her daughter, "what time you finish practice?"

"Oh, I guess around two, two thirty," answered Dana, adjusting her bright red team cap, wearing it so low that she could barely see. After all, this was just the way Jeremy Catelli, the best player on the team, wore his.

"Okay, we be back and meet you here," Dana's mother told Dana, pointing to the clubhouse fence.

"Hit a homer for me, Princess!" yelled Chuck, grinning his wide smile as he drove past Dana.

Dana slowly walked toward the clubhouse, since there

was still over an hour to kill. Dana noticed as she walked over the narrow cement asphalt and onto the dirt court-yard that there were not any birds chirping. Usually, despite the Richmond District fog, Dana could hear the tiny song birds singing their pretty little songs by the apple trees. There would be about three or four gathering together upon the highest branch of the tallest of the three apple trees. During the sizzling days of Indian summer, Dana and some of her teammates would climb the trees and pick the greenest apples they could find. Of course, Dana would take a few home for her mother to taste. But on this cold May morning, not only were there no birds, there were no ripe apples, either. This seemed to add to the overall morbidness of the park, a kind of still silence Dana thought quite odd, especially on a Saturday.

As Dana neared the clubhouse, she was careful not to step on the cracks of the cement blocks that were laid on the clubhouse yard. It was an old habit of hers, a game she played when she was bored.

"Well, hello there!" a voice sprang out of nowhere. Dana's head immediately lifted up from looking at the asphalt squares. Out of the clubhouse walked Coach Getty in his usual faded light-blue Levi's and his red wind-breaker team jacket. The windbreaker still had a ripped left pocket; Coach Getty had not sewn it up since Dana had started playing Little League four years ago. A burly man, Coach Getty stood an average five feet ten inches tall and looked as if he could lift a tow truck. Although he denied ever lifting weights, the kids on the team knew better. No one knew exactly what Coach Getty kept in the clubhouse, but rumor had it that there were sets of weights stacked high enough to make Hulk Hogan whimper. There he was, standing in his usual stance, arms crossed against his wide chest, feet apart, and smoking his famous Tiparillo miniature cigar. The Tiparillos were his favorite. "A real man's cigar," he used to say.

"You scared the hell out of me, Coach," Dana said, trying to calm her jumpy nerves. She noticed as she looked up at him that she still had her cap down at her eyes. Trying to look a bit more ladylike, she took off her cap and straightened out her pressed hair. Dana tried not to look too obvious as she looked down at her feet, kicking from side to side the tiny rocks left on the rough asphalt. It was important to her that Coach Getty see she was serious about baseball and that she was not one of many girls her age who cared only about their appearance. Admittedly, however, Dana did care about her looks, as any fourteen-year-old girl would. In fact, she had just started to experiment with her mother's eye liner, only to smear it all off before anyone could see her.

"Oh, I hope I didn't startle you too bad. Did you lose something there?" Coach Getty asked, sucking the smoke from his Tiparillo. "Looks like you lost something valuable." The strong scent from the Tiparillo had never smelled so strangely sweet to Dana. What she usually thought of as a rancid stink was now a smooth and soft scent that gave Dana a feeling of comfort and warmth, as if she were somehow accepted by someone dear. Coach Getty was indeed dear to Dana. It was only until now, however, that Dana had felt this sense of appreciation.

"No, I just try to avoid stepping on the little cracks. It's a silly game I play," Dana replied, giving her hair one last stroke back, not realizing there was a pretty shine bouncing off her golden hair strands.

"Oh, it's not all that silly," Coach Getty told her. "In fact, I still play the game. That is, when you kids aren't watching me." Coach Getty tried to reassure the sometimes dubious Dana. Coach Getty knew that unlike the boys on the team, Dana was an emotional balloon waiting to burst. Not only did she seem to get down on herself more than any of the other players, but she would dwell on her faults longer than anyone else, longer than necessary. Coach Getty liked her hard-work ethics on the field, and they had certainly helped her win a starting position as their first baseman. But she was too hard on herself. A missed ground ball would haunt the fragile-minded Dana until next week's game. Coach Getty knew this weakness, this self-destructive force, and as a result chose his words carefully. He was always careful with Dana.

"My, you're early today, aren't you?" Coach Getty asked, not necessarily expecting an answer. "You know, practice doesn't start 'til noon."

"Oh, I know. But my mom and her boyfriend had to go do some other things, so they dropped me off here. I told them it was okay with you and that I could even help around," Dana told Coach Getty, wanting desperately to be his assistant.

"Why, that's real sweet of you, Dana. I think I'll take you up on that," Coach Getty said, appearing pleased at the idea that Dana wanted to help. As he inhaled another puff from his Tiparillo, and as Dana set down her backpack to put on her cleats, Coach Getty noticed how pretty she was. Her hair gave her an air of innocence and gentleness, which was hardly noticed by others in the tomboyish Dana. He felt satisfaction in observing her soft facial skin, skin that was so delicately colored a light shade of pink that it went perfectly with her shiny hair. He began to see in her a maturing young lady. Each summer, Coach Getty had the pleasure of watching his little female superstar develop into something beautiful, all so naturally. Dana was gradually becoming a young woman.

Finally, Coach Getty had to say something to the ostensibly occupied Dana. "Hey, Dana," he called as Dana got through with tying her left cleat, "your hair is beginning to look real nice nowadays. Are you doing anything different to it?" Coach Getty asked as if he had a sincere interest in whether or not Dana did do something different to her hair.

"No," Dana replied a bit puzzled, yet undeniably flattered. In actuality, she had done something different to her hair. With the help of her girl friend, Kerry, she had learned how to style it with a curling iron. But never was she going to let Coach Getty know of this. No, he would think it too sissy. Dana had to prove that she was just as tough as the next guy, for she loved playing on the team and it was important to her to play well. Obviously, playing well meant becoming accepted by her pals, and of course, by Coach Getty.

"Why?" Dana finally asked, as if she really did not know why Coach Getty even mentioned such a frivolous thing as her hair. But she was excited that someone was paying attention, since none of the boys in school ever said anything. To them Dana was just another boy. She played baseball in the summer and basketball in the winter just like the boys. She even avoided the Madison Junior High dances, because she knew that none of the boys would dance with someone who could out-play them in sports. But Coach Getty was different from the boys at Madison Junior High. He noticed Dana for who she was and what she was becoming, even if Dana did not fully know herself.

"It just looks real nice, that's all. You're beginning to look real pretty," Coach Getty said, complimenting her. He felt a great sense of emotional release by saying that. He knew the oversensitive Dana and was ambivalent as to how she would react. She was pretty, and he was beginning to think fondly of his young star first baseman. Unsurprisingly, Coach Getty's comment made Dana blush. Her light-pink facial color deepened into a bright-red shade, and her hazel eyes sparkled. Coach Getty knew then to change the subject immediately, for it created a silence between the two.

"Hey, do you still need help with that swing of yours?" he asked in a feeble attempt to steer the conversation away from her appearance. "You haven't been doing too well at the plate, and if you want to improve that swing, now is the time to ask."

"Sure," Dana agreed, "I could use some pointers to help the slump I'm in." Dana began walking toward Coach Getty, who could not help eyeing Dana. The clubhouse door was half open, which was unusual as he did not like anyone to see what was in "his room." Dana tried to sneak a quick look inside, but to no avail, as Coach Getty towered over her, blocking any view of the clubhouse.

"Now," he began, grabbing a thirty-two-inch Louisville Slugger from the black Converse bat bag, "this is what I want you to do. I want you to hold the bat as you normally would and stand in the batting stance that you're comfortable with."

Dana listened attentively and did as she was instructed. "Like this?" she asked. She wanted to please him. She wanted to impress him with her willingness to learn. Coach Getty made her feel special. Dana was finally getting the attention that she always found so difficult to get around the boys.

"That's it, Dana. Now, swing in slow motion as you would when the ball's being pitched."

As Dana's arms slowly swung forward with the bat, she noticed that Coach Getty's chest was touching her back. She felt a bit awkward. She had never been so close to him before. However, with Coach Getty she felt the same sense of protection and security she did with Chuck. Dana continued her motion. By the time she had finished her swing, though, Dana felt Coach Getty's hands gently holding her waist. Coach Getty had stopped giving instructions. He had stopped talked altogether as his hands gradually began to touch her.

She was scared. The world and everything in it froze. Dana truly became aware of the silence of the birds, the sweet birds that were usually so loud. What is happening?

she wondered. He cannot be doing what I think he is doing, she thought. Still, Coach Getty's hands continued to fondle her.

Bewildered and frightened even more, Dana stood still. She could not believe what was taking place. This is my coach, Dana thought to herself. He cannot be trying to touch me. Dana felt numb. . . .

Finally, Dana had enough courage to break away from the ironlike arms of Coach Getty. Enough was enough. She quickly ran to her gym bag, throwing her mitt into the dark, deep corners of the bag where she wanted to be.

Stomping away from the clubhouse courtyard, Dana felt immense anger and betrayal. "Are ya gonna tell?" Coach Getty howled after her like a wolf. There was even an audacious layer of sarcasm to Coach Getty's voice. Dana had no time to analyze Coach Getty's words, tone, or intentions. She felt that she had to leave. She had to see her mother. She had to see Chuck.

"Maybe, maybe not," Dana replied half-heartedly. Dana wondered why those words of ambiguity spouted from her mouth as she threw her backpack over her shoulders and ran past the metal gates that separated the clubhouse and Evans Field. Dana did not know what she meant exactly by her own reply. She could not believe, much less understand, what had just happened.

And yet . . . Coach Getty was such an icon of protection, knowledge, and experience to her. How could she speak out against him? All the words of outrage stopped at her lips. It was impossible to say anything.

"Why you back so early?" Dana's mother asked, surprised and startled as Dana slammed the apartment door behind her. Chuck and Dana's mother were kneeling on the kitchen floor taping up the cardboard boxes full of plates and cups.

With her baseball-cap bill almost at eye level, Dana quickly darted into her empty room, saying only, "Practice was canceled." Bewildered, Chuck and Dana's mother looked at each other while the clicking of the push-button lock on Dana's bedroom door echoed against the pictureless kitchen walls.

"What's the matter, Princess?" Chuck asked curiously, knocking on Dana's door. Dana's mother returned to sticking the last strip of tape on the cardboard box, but Chuck felt that Dana's abrupt answer and behavior was a bit eccentric. He had never seen such a confused and worried look on Dana's face.

"Nothing. Just go away . . . please," Dana said hesitantly.

"What's wrong, Dana?" Chuck repeated. "What happened?"

There was silence.

"Is everything all right?" Chuck tried again to get an answer from Dana. "What do you think is the matter with Dana, honey?" Chuck asked, turning to Dana's mother.

"Oh, she be okay," Dana's mother assured Chuck. "You know Dana. You know she no talk sometimes."

Reluctantly, Chuck gave up. He was dissatisfied by Dana's mother's quick dismissal of Dana's behavior. Yet he could not interfere in a "family affair" or a "mother-daughter" conflict. Helplessly he stared at Dana's door.

Inside her "castle," however, Dana was begging for solace. She could not withhold her tears. As she huddled her small frame against the corner of her room where her single futon used to lie, Dana sobbed uncontrollably. She was a vortex of hurt. Dana rested her head on her kneecaps as she sat on the cold linoleum floor, the base of her spine pressing tightly against the dark plaster of the adjoining two walls. Not having any tissues, Dana wiped away tears on the sleeves of her team jacket.

Dana tried to endure the pain by herself. She tried to hold it in inside. But soon after she knew she wasn't up to the struggle. She needed to tell someone. She needed to tell her mother.

"It will make me feel better," Dana assured herself. "Besides, it will bring us a lot closer," she added hopefully.

All her life, she had tried to win her mother's acceptance, but the two constantly clashed. Much to Dana's dismay, they were at two different ends of every spectrum.

But Dana was going to change all that. For once her mother would have to pay attention to her daughter and accept Dana for the emotional way she was, and not the stoic way that her mother wanted her to be. Dana waited until the next morning.

"Mom, I need to talk to you," Dana said, walking to the kitchen sink as her mother washed out the soybean jars. Dana's mother never threw anything away, and she used the soybean jars to store other food items. Her mother did not answer. Continuing her scrubbing of the insides of the jars, Dana's mother just nodded her head. Dana knew that this was her way of saying, "Yes, what is it, dear?" the way any "caring" mother would reply.

"Remember last Saturday when I came in and said that practice was canceled?" asked Dana, feeling unusually confident, yet a bit nervous. There was no oral response by her mother. Dana continued, nonetheless. "Well, practice wasn't canceled. I just came home. Something happened with Coach Getty." Feeling more nervous now than confident, Dana reluctantly continued talking. "I was alone with him practicing on my swing and . . ." Suddenly, Dana could not go on. Still, she knew that she had to. It was just that her mother's lack of vocal acknowledgment toward Dana's expressing herself, coupled with her lack of eye contact, was not making this any easier on Dana. She could not believe the lack of attentiveness displayed by her mother. She took a deep breath and decided once and for all to tell her mother the conclusion of what had happened that Saturday morning. "He felt my private area, Mom," Dana finally said, as her mother suddenly stopped soaking the soybean jars in the sudsy soap water.

"What you mean?" Dana's mother asked, confused.

Dana was surprised by her mother's sudden interest. Encouraged, she went on, "He touched me all over, Mommy. I couldn't believe what he was doing to me, but I was too scared to do anything about it. Please don't tell Chuck. I feel so ashamed. Coach Getty just started to hold my waist and then he started touching my chest. I didn't know what was happening at first, but when I felt funny, I ran away."

Dana felt an unbelievable sense of relief—as though a twenty-pound bag of potatoes had been lifted off her shoulders. The pain was still there, but Dana no longer felt alone.

However, Dana's mother did not say anything. Much to Dana's shock, she just turned back toward the sink and began rinsing the soybean jars again.

"Why you go to practice so early, you dummy? You no think many men that way? You no careful, that why, Dana." The soybean jars were now clanging against one another as Dana's mother began to run the water at full speed and rinse them as fast as she could. She was obviously highly upset.

"What do you mean, Mom?" Dana asked, confused and bewildered at her mother's reaction. "It wasn't my fault. It was his fault." Dana could not believe, much less understand, that she needed to justify her actions to her mother.

"You know better now than to go to practice so early. You so stupid to go and act like little girl, knowing nothing, shaking ass all around." Her mother's voice was accusing. By this time she had shut off the faucet and begun to dry off the soybean jars with the pink-strawberry-design dish towel. This was unusual. Her mother never towel dried dishes. She always set the dishes in the dish drain and let them air dry. Dana saw that she had made her mother extremely uncomfortable. Dana had done it again. She had gotten her mother upset. This time, however, Dana knew that she had gotten her mother angrier than ever. She just did not know how or why.

Dana ran into her room, her castle, but it seemed more

dismal and morbid than ever before. Dana seemed more alone than ever before. No one in the world knew what she was feeling. No one. Tears started to roll down her face, hugging her flushed red cheeks—the color that told of anger, frustration, and hopelessness.

"It's not my fault! It's not my fault!" Dana yelled to herself, but not loud enough for her mother to have heard in the kitchen. Dana's tears were uncontrollable. She sobbed for what felt like days, weeks, months. "I am not a slut! I never wanted this! I wish I were dead and I bet my own mother could care less!"

Dana lay down on the dusty floor of her room and cried unceasingly. Her head felt as though it was holding all the world's pain. It was too much for an adult to handle, much less a fourteen-year-old girl. "I want to die," Dana cried out in agony. She would rather kill herself and end this pain than go through life feeling this hurt and having to face the people who had hurt her. She wished it had never happened.

Dana woke up the next morning with a severe case of the chills. Having fallen asleep without a blanket the night before, Dana felt cold. Folding her arms around herself, Dana wished that the previous night had all been a dream, a very bad dream. A glance at the mirror that was still screwed to the back of the bedroom door, however, revealed her swollen eyes, a result not of a bad dream but of grim reality. She felt guilty for something she had no control over. Dana hated herself.

Suddenly she saw the half-open cardboard box. The heads of her cherished unicorns peeked out of the rumpled *Archie* pages. Hatred filled her eyes. "Lies! All lies!" Dana yelled, immediately getting up and tearing open the wrapped unicorns. Grabbing the family of unicorns, Dana threw them against the ugly brown floor. Thousands of little pieces of glass scattered in all directions. "I hate you little bastards! You mean nothing to me!" Dana raged. "So much for family. There's no such thing. Nobody cares for no one."

"Why did you lie to me?" Dana asked the father unicorn, his head and body shattered. And with them went all the innocence and beauty of the world.

"Unicorns don't even exist. Not in my eyes." In Dana's eyes, nothing good existed, not anymore, not ever again.

The Wise Child

The children of immigrant parents learn to grow up fast because they frequently find themselves acting as their own parents' interpreters. It would not be unusual to have a five-year-old child transacting business with a UPS delivery person. The dependency of Asian American parents upon their offspring gives the children a kind of double vision—not only of their parents but of the Hopescape itself. Judith Nihei has used this double perspective to good effect in her bittersweet "Koden."

Adolescence is normally a time when teenagers try to step out of their parents' long shadows. Inevitably, they feel like rebels creating a new order. Janice Mirikitani's poem "Breaking Tradition" humorously points out what happens when one of these teenage revolutionaries grows up.

Even conscientious parents can have trouble adjusting to the changes in their children as they grow up. In her essay "A Sea Worry," Maxine Hong Kingston describes a parent trying to understand her surfer son.

The talented JUDITH NIHEI is a Japanese American who wears an impressive number of creative hats. As an actor, she has appeared in films such as Living on Tokyo Time. *As a comic, she does improvisations each week with the satiric group The National Theater of the Deranged. As a director, she has worked on many important Asian American plays. Her many theatrical skills have brought a keenness of observation to her writing.*

KODEN

I guess you could say I was having a bad year. If you asked me to tell you why, I probably couldn't. Or maybe I could say a lot of things but they wouldn't mean anything to anyone but me. A lot of people say they want to know, but I'm not sure if they really do or not.

I was supposed to be doing a lot of things. I was supposed to get my driver's license and I was supposed to start thinking about college and I was supposed to be, I don't know, moody and difficult. I was moody, I guess, but I think the only difficult thing about me was that I wasn't being difficult. I didn't want anything. I didn't refuse what I was given, and I spoke when I was spoken to, and I kept my grades up. I quit softball and piano lessons, but everyone was expecting me to do that anyway.

I did get a second hole pierced in my left ear, which no

one can even see if my hair is down and two holes in one ear is nothing compared with what some people at my school are doing. But my dad never wanted me to get my ears pierced in the first place, so I guess it really burned him that I hadn't even asked before I got the second hole done. I might have discussed it with him if I hadn't felt like I had to have an army of lawyers to prove my case every time I disagreed with him. Not that he yells. He just slowly and quietly convinces you how wrong you are.

"You don't think," he'd say, which really hurt because it felt like I was thinking all the time—like I could be who they wanted me to be if only I could *stop* thinking. And if I got mad, he'd get even more annoyed.

"Don't get so upset," he would say. "No big deal."

Anyway, the day Kenny died, my mom was still at work and I'd just gotten home from school when Dad called.

"Hello?"

"Yeah," he said. "This is Dad."

"Hi," I said. "Mom's not home yet."

He cleared his throat. "You know, in life there is both happiness and sorrow."

I could almost see him holding the phone, standing with his head up, shoulders back, throwing out his chest like he did when he'd show us how he delivered his big speech for the Japanese School program when he was twelve. I couldn't believe it. He was performing for me.

Who died? I wanted to ask. Somebody's dead. Grandma had a bad heart and Grandpa was always wandering around by himself with his cane. At my brother's graduation the summer before, when I'd had my picture taken with them, I got a funny feeling that if I went away to college in a couple of years, I might not be home when they died, that I might not be home for a lot of things.

"Yeah," I said, "so—?"

"Kenny's dead," he said.

I was so surprised that I actually shouted into the phone, which is something you never did to my dad.

"WHAT?"

My cousin Kenny had been the next Umetsu to be born after me. Russ and I were the oldest cousins and our dad was the oldest brother. Then came Uncle Ben, Uncle Jack, Uncle Ed and Uncle Bill. The first wedding I remember going to was when Uncle Ben, Kenny's father, married Auntie Harumi. The reason I remember it so well is because the whole time my mom was getting mad at me for scratching and fussing my way through the wedding ceremony, and the thing was she had left some pins in my dress when she made it. Kenny was their first-born son. He had just turned twelve.

"It was an accident," my dad said.

The day of the funeral I ended up waiting for my brother on the bench outside the main doors of my school. My parents had taken the day off to go over to the East Bay early, but I wasn't supposed to have my education disrupted. Anyway, they were making Russ come back for me. He was in his first year at Berkeley, and I knew he wasn't going to be happy about having to drive across the Bay to get me and then drive all the way back, but that was his tough luck for being born first.

I stood up just in time to see the pale-yellow Volkswagen Bug maneuver toward the curb. The car pulled up, and Russ leaned over and opened the passenger door from the inside. I threw my bag into the backseat, got inside and slammed the door shut. All the windows were closed, and the pressure thudded in my ear.

Auntie Harumi used to say that Russell and I were like two cats forced to share a territory, glaring and avoiding, showing our claws from a distance, occasionally hissing and spitting and mixing it up. This last year it had mostly been avoiding. The scratch marks had become scars. We didn't talk much.

When we got through Golden Gate Park, he downshifted and we exited into the busy traffic on Fell Street, stopping at the light by the DMV. It was suddenly quiet enough for me to feel my ears tingling from the noise. Russell played with the knob of the gearshift, jiggling it from side to side in neutral. The quiet bothered me.

"How is everybody?" I asked.

"I haven't really talked to Auntie and Uncle yet," he said, staring at the light. "I think everybody's pretty upset. Do you know how it happened?"

"No," I said, "do you?"

"Yeah."

"Who told you?"

"Dad."

"Figures."

"Grow up. This isn't about you."

"So tell me, then."

"Kenny was playing in their backyard. The kids had this rope and they were up in that big tree and Kenny slipped."

"And hit his head?"

"And hanged himself," Russell said, pounding into first gear as the light changed to green.

I guess no one told me because they thought I would cry or something, which is something you never do in front of my parents. I think Russell thought I was going to cry, too, but I never cry in front of anyone anymore.

"Where are we going?" I said instead.

"Grandma and Grandpa's. So you'd better keep your hair over those ears."

I didn't know what was going to happen. I had only been to one funeral before, when my mom's father died, and I was really little then so all I remembered was the smell of the Buddhist incense and the sleepy drone of the priest chanting. My father's family were Presbyterians, so I knew there wouldn't be any chanting or anything, but I thought that might make it worse because then you could understand everything. When we got to the funeral parlor on the night of the service and I saw the table, I did remember the *koden*.

It was a small oak table in the middle of the lobby. I saw my Uncle Ed, representing our family, sitting behind it next to one of Auntie Harumi's brothers, who represented theirs. As people came in, they'd stop and put a white envelope in front of Uncle Ed. Sometimes it was the size of a greeting card, and sometimes it was long and narrow and covered with Japanese characters. Uncle Ed thanked everybody, nodding or sharing hands, sometimes cracking jokes like he does, which seemed kind of weird although I guess it really wasn't. Then he'd hand the envelope to Auntie's brother, who put in a covered, lacquered box, like the kind Grandma used for sushi on New Year's Day.

I knew this was the *koden*, the money. In each envelope was anywhere from five to fifty dollars. I had seen my parents get their envelopes ready for other funerals—my mom writing their name and address on the envelope because her handwriting was better, my dad making sure that the five-, ten- or twenty-dollar bill was crisp and new.

"What's the money for?" I asked my mom once.

"It's a custom," she said.

I wanted to know what they did with the money and she said sometimes they used it to pay for the funeral and sometimes they gave it away to people who really needed it, like the cancer society. When I asked my dad why they gave *koden*, he said it was out of respect.

The funeral was sad, and I'm still not sure what I think about that. They buried Kenny the next day. The people who came to the burial were invited to my uncle and aunt's house, and all of a sudden everyone was busy—making food and unfolding chairs and shaking hands. Being the oldest, my dad took charge, like he always does, greeting people and thanking people, like this was no different from any other big family party. Russ played with the cousins, and the uncles made drinks and took care of our grandparents, and the aunts cooked and served and washed all the dishes twice. It seemed like everyone had something to do and someone to be except me.

It was the most time I had spent with the family in a long time, and I don't know, it was different. I felt like I'd lost my place in a favorite book I'd been rereading, that each page was familiar but I couldn't quite find the exact place where I needed to be. I stood as long as I could in one spot and then sat in one chair or another until I felt like standing up again.

Finally, just the family was left and it was time to clear the dining-room table. Uncle Jack went out to his car and brought back two brand-new notebooks and some pens and pencils. He gave them to me to put on the table, where someone had already replaced the punch bowls and salami and sushi with an adding machine, a shoe box and the lacquer box from the night before. There were six chairs, two on each side and one on either end. My dad sat at one end, with Teri, Uncle Jack's wife, on his left and my mom on his right. Uncle Bill's wife, Sue, sat next to her and Uncle Bill sat at the other end, with the adding machine in front of him. Someone turned down the volume of the TV in the next room, and then it was time to count the *koden*.

Auntie Teri had the lacquer box open in front of her. She took out an envelope, wrote a number on it and handed it to Dad. He opened it.

"Mrs. Yoneko Omi. Ten dollars."

Mom wrote the name and amount in her notebook each time Dad spoke. He handed the card to her and she recorded its number, then gave the envelope to Auntie Sue, Bill's wife, who was sitting at her right. In a book like mom's, Auntie Sue recorded the address if there was one. She then stored the card or envelope in a shoe box and handed the money or check to Uncle Bill, who kept a running tally on the adding machine.

"Motomo and Edna Ishigashi. Twenty dollars."

I wandered into the kitchen. Auntie Harumi was swinging a large pan of chow mein out of the oven. I watched her pour the noodles onto a platter and spread the vegetables over the top with her chopsticks, standing at a distance to keep the sauce from splattering her neat black dress.

"Hey, how's it going out there?" she asked.

"Okay, I guess. Um, how are you doing?"

Auntie Harumi wiped her hands on a dish towel.

"Oh, okay. It'll be different when everybody goes home, but for now . . ."

She dropped her voice and took my arm, looking over my shoulder to make sure no one else would hear.

". . . you know, while you're here, I want to tell you something."

"What?"

"I told your uncle—"

"Which one?"

"My husband, smart aleck. I told your Uncle Ben, I said, 'Your family is the best.' Gee, your dad-folks are just taking care of everything. Auntie's family is here, huh? But they're not lifting a finger."

"That's because Dad won't let them," I said.

Auntie laughed. She reached over and pushed my hair behind my ears.

"Oh, you got a second hole. Neat!"

I let the hair fall back onto into my face.

"Dad had a cow," I said.

"Not happy," she said, smiling.

"I waited until last year to even ask if I could have my ears pierced. I think Mom was on my side, but . . . you know. So I figured, they're my ears—"

Auntie laughed again.

"You and your dad," she said. "You know, he was always the different one."

"My dad?"

"He grew this beard once, and your grandmother had a fit! She thought it was the most horrible thing she had ever seen, couldn't stand to have any of her friends see him like that."

"Dad had a beard?"

"Oh, long time ago—before Ben and I were even dating. I remember her coming over to our house and almost apologizing to my mother, because no matter what she said, he wouldn't shave it off."

"Well it's gone now."

"Yeah, but not because anyone told him to get rid of it. Your dad has his own mind. Just like you."

I walked back into the dining room and stood behind

my dad's chair. Work at the table went on slowly, methodically. I watched and waited for a break in the rhythm. Finally they stopped so that Mom could turn the page of her notebook.

"Can I get anybody anything?" I asked. They all shifted in their seats and stretched. Auntie Teri sipped her coffee and made a face.

"Cold," she said.

She picked up her cup and headed for the kitchen, where we could hear Uncle Ben and Uncle Jack arguing over someone's golf handicap. Auntie Sue walked around the table and took Auntie Teri's place. Uncle Ed wandered in with a glass in his hand and sat in Sue's empty seat. Mom took off her glasses and massaged her eyes.

"Yeah," my dad said. "Why don't you give Mom a break, there."

Mom stood up, pressed her hands to the small of her back and walked toward the kitchen. I looked down at her place, and Uncle Ed shifted to his right. I sat down and pulled the chair closer to the table. I picked up the ballpoint pen Mom had been using. It was warm. I looked at the notebook to see where she was, the number where she'd stopped. I wiped my hand on my thigh and moved her coffee cup way beyond where it could do any harm.

"Ready?" Dad asked.

I nodded and the rhythm began again.

"Tominaga. Harry and Alice. Twenty-five dollars."

I wrote. He glanced at my writing. He repeated:

"Tominaga. Harry and Alice. Twenty-five dollars."

He handed me the envelope. I checked the number

and I handed it to my uncle.

"The Mas Ninomiya Family. Twenty-five dollars. . . ."

We worked from twilight to darkness. My grandparents were taken upstairs to rest. I blended into the rhythm and pattern of the table, until at last it was finished.

It was almost nine o'clock. My dad never did take a break. He gave the box of money to Auntie Harumi's brother-in-law, who was an accountant, and asked him to please count it again to be sure that the total was correct. While everyone else was stretching and gathering up their things, I handed my notebook to my dad so that he could double-check it. I knew if any money was lost or anything, he would question my work first, but he just took it and placed it on the table with the rest.

"How about a cup of coffee?" he asked.

I turned to go to the kitchen, but he placed his hand gently on my arm.

"Ayako," he called to my mom, "how about bringing us some coffee?"

He opened the French doors that led to the backyard, and we stepped outside. The fog was coming in from the Bay, rolling through the top of the tree where Kenny had been playing. Its coolness made me realize how warm I had been. My dad reached into his shirt pocket and pulled out a new pack of cigarettes. He tore off the cellophane wrapper and tore into the foil. He tapped the pack against his left hand so that two cigarettes poked out, and then he offered one to me.

I shook my head.

"I don't smoke, Dad."

"Well, that's something."

He pulled one out for himself and lit it with his heavy square lighter, cupping his hand around the flame against the wind.

"Maybe we ought to cut this tree down," he said, squinting through the smoke at the big tree.

"Why?"

"I don't know. I guess it's not the tree's fault."

"Maybe it would make Auntie and Uncle feel better, though."

"I don't know what could help them feel better. Your kids aren't supposed to die before you do."

When I was little and we spent every Sunday at our grandparents' house, playing with our uncles before they married and had their own families, I thought my father and his brothers were an unbeatable force. But as the day of the funeral had approached, they had been different, shaky, like they had to fight to stay in charge, like it was their fault, somehow, that they couldn't protect Kenny, prevent it from happening.

I didn't know what to say, so I shoved my hair behind my ears and then covered them up as soon as I realized what I'd done. I looked away.

"Do you want your coffee out here, Dad? I'll go get it."

Instead of answering, he put his hand on my head and turned it toward him. I looked up at him, and he pushed my hair back behind my ears.

"I like to see your face," he said.

I couldn't help it. I started to cry then, which really

made me mad because I knew it would upset him. But instead of telling me to stop, Dad put his arm around me, which made me cry even more. After a while I kind of stopped and he gave me his handkerchief.

"I'm sorry, Daddy," I said.

"No big deal," he said, lighting another cigarette. "Go inside now. It's getting cold."

Dad turned away from me then, walking deeper into the yard toward my brother and my cousins, and I watched the tip of his cigarette glow in the darkness, floating like a small torch in the dark night.

Though she is Japanese American, JANICE MIRIKITANI's poem deals with a situation familiar to any Asian American parents—or parents in general.

Otonashii means quiet and good-tempered. A shakuhachi is a bamboo flute.

BREAKING TRADITION
for my Daughter

My daughter denies she is like me,
her secretive eyes avoid mine.
    She reveals the hatreds of womanhood
    already veiled behind music and smoke and telephones.
I want to tell her about the empty room
    of myself.
    This room we lock ourselves in
    where whispers live like fungus,
    giggles about small breasts and cellulite,
    where we confine ourselves to jealousies,
    bedridden by menstruation.
    This waiting room where we feel our hands
    are useless, dead speechless clamps
    that need hospitals and forceps and kitchens
    and plugs and ironing boards to make them useful.
I deny I am like my mother. I remember why:
    She kept her room neat with silence,
    defiance smothered in requirements to be otonashii,
    passion and loudness wrapped in an obi,

her steps confined to ceremony,
the weight of her sacrifice she carried like
a foetus. Guilt passed on in our bones.
I want to break tradition—unlock this room
where women dress in the dark.
Discover the lies my mother told me.
The lies that we are small and powerless
that our possibilities must be compressed
to the size of pearls, displayed only as
passive chokers, charms around our neck.
Break Tradition.
I want to tell my daughter of this room
of myself
filled with tears of shakuhachi,
the light in my hands,
poems about madness,
the music of yellow guitars—
sounds shaken from barbed wire and
goodbyes and miracles of survival.
My daughter denies she is like me
her secretive eyes are walls of smoke
and music and telephones,
her pouting ruby lips, her skirts
swaying to salsa, Madonna and the Stones,
her thighs displayed in carnavals of color.
I do not know the contents of her room.
She mirrors my aging.
She is breaking tradition.

MAXINE HONG KINGSTON *is a Chinese American writer most famous for her novels* The Woman Warrior, China Men *and* Tripmaster Monkey.

A SEA WORRY

This summer my son body-surfs. He says it's his "job" and rises each morning at 5:30 to catch the bus to Sandy Beach. I hope that by September he will have had enough of the ocean. Tall waves throw surfers against the shallow bottom. Undertows have snatched them away. Sharks prowl Sandy's. Joseph told me that once he got out of the water because he saw an enormous shark. "Did you tell the lifeguard?" I asked. "No." "Why not?" "I didn't want to spoil the surfing." The ocean pulls at the boys, who turn into surfing addicts. At sunset you can see the surfers waiting for the last golden wave.

"Why do you go surfing so often?" I ask my students.

"It feels so good," they say. "Inside the tube, I can't describe it. There are no words for it."

"You can describe it," I scold, and I am very angry. "Everything can be described. Find the words for it, you lazy boy. Why don't you go home and read?" I am afraid that the boys give themselves up to the ocean's mindlessness.

When the waves are up, surfers all over Hawaii don't do their homework. They cut school. They know how the surf is breaking at any moment because every fifteen minutes the reports come over the radio; in fact, one of my former students is the surf reporter.

Some boys leave for mainland colleges, and write their parents heartrending letters. They beg to come home for Thanksgiving. "If I can just touch the ocean," they write from Missouri and Kansas, "I'll last for the rest of the semester." Some come home for Christmas and don't go back.

Even when the assignment is about something else, the students write about surfing. They try to describe what it is to be inside the wave as it curls over them, making a tube or "chamber" or "green room" or "pipeline" or "time warp." They write about the silence, the peace, "no hassles," the feeling of being reborn as they shoot out the end. They've written about the perfect wave. Their writing is full of clichés. "The endless summer," they say. "Unreal."

Surfing is like a religion. Among the martyrs are George Helm, Kimo Mitchell, and Eddie Aikau. Helm and Mitchell were lost at sea riding their surfboards from Kaho'olawe, where they had gone to protest the Navy's bombing of that island. Eddie Aikau was a champion surfer and lifeguard. A storm had capsized the *Hokule'a*, the ship that traced the route that the Polynesian ancestors sailed from Tahiti, and Eddie Aikau had set out on his board to get help.

Since the ocean captivates our son, we decided to go with him to Sandy's.

We got up before dawn, picked up his friend, Marty, and drove out of Honolulu. Almost all the traffic was going in the opposite direction, the freeway coned to make more lanes into the city. We came to a place where raw mountains rose on our left and the sea fell on our right, smashing against the cliffs. The strip of cliff pulverized into sand is Sandy's. "Dangerous Current Exist," said the ungrammatical sign.

Earll and I sat on the shore with our blankets and thermos of coffee. Joseph and Marty put on their fins and stood at the edge of the sea for a moment, touching the water with their fingers and crossing their hearts before going in. There were fifteen boys out there, all about the same age, fourteen to twenty, all with the same kind of lean v-shaped build, most of them with black hair that made their wet heads look like sea lions. It was hard to tell whether our kid was one of those who popped up after a big wave. A few had surfboards, which are against the rules at a body-surfing beach, but the lifeguard wasn't on duty that day.

As they watched for the next wave, the boys turned toward the ocean. They gazed slightly upward; I thought of altar boys before a great god. When a good wave arrived, they turned, faced shore, and came shooting in, some taking the wave to the right and some to the left, their bodies fish-like, one arm out in front, the hand and fingers pointed before them, like a swordfish's beak. A few held credit card trays, and some slid in on trays from MacDonald's.

"That is no country for middle-aged women," I said. We had on bathing suits underneath our clothes in case we felt moved to participate. There were no older men either.

Even from the shore, we could see inside the tubes. Sometimes, when they came at an angle, we saw into them a long way. When the wave dug into the sand, it formed a brown tube or a golden one. The magic ones, though, were made out of just water, green and turquoise rooms, translucent walls and ceilings. I saw one that was powder-blue, perfect, thin; the sun filled it with sky blue and white light. The best thing, the kids say, is when you are in the middle of the tube, and there is water all around you but you're dry.

The waves came in sets; the boys passed up the smaller ones. Inside a big one, you could see their bodies hanging upright, knees bent, duckfeet fins paddling, bodies dangling there in the wave.

Once in a while, we heard a boy yell, "Aa-whoo!" "Poon-tah!" "Aaroo!" And then we noticed how rare a human voice was here; the surfers did not talk, but silently, silently rode the waves.

Since Joseph and Marty were considerate of us, they stopped after two hours, and we took them out for breakfast. We kept asking them how it felt, so they would not lose language.

"Like a stairwell in an apartment building," said Joseph, which I liked immensely. He hasn't been in very many apartment buildings, so had to reach a bit to get the simile. "I saw somebody I knew coming toward me in the tube, and I shouted, 'Jeff. Hey, Jeff,' and my voice echoed like a stairwell in an apartment building. Jeff and I came straight at each other—mirror tube."

"Are there ever girls out there?" Earll asked.

"There's a few who come out at about eleven," said Marty.

"How old are they?"

"About twenty."

"Why do you cross your heart with water?"

"So the ocean doesn't kill us."

I describe the powder-blue tube I had seen. "That part of Sandy's is called Chambers," they said.

I have gotten some surfing magazines, the ones kids steal from the school library, to see if the professionals try to describe the tube.

Bradford Baker writes:

> . . . Round and pregnant in Emptiness
>   I slide,
>   Laughing,
>   into the sun,
>   into the night.

Frank Miller calls the surfer

> . . . mother's fumbling
>   curly-haired
>   tubey-laired
>   son.

"Ooh, offshores—" writes Reno Abbellira, "where wind and wave most often form that terminal rendezvous of love—when the wave can reveal her deepest longings, her crest caressed, cannily covered to form those peeling concavities we know, perhaps a bit irreverently, as tubes. Here we strive to spend every second—enclosed, en-

cased, sometimes fatefully entombed, and hopefully, glee-
fully ejected—Whoosh!"

"An iridescent ride through the entrails of God," says
Gary L. Crandall.

I am relieved that the surfers keep asking one another
for descriptions. I also find some comfort in the stream of
commuter traffic, cars filled with men over twenty, passing Sandy Beach on their way to work.

World War Two

In the American Hopescape lies a seared area created by a shameful period in American history. After Pearl Harbor, Japanese Americans were made to feel like criminals because of their ancestry. Richard Haratani's "Attention to Detail" describes the nightmare for many Japanese Americans at the start of World War Two.

By presidential order, Japanese Americans were forcibly evacuated from the coast and taken inland. Because they were allowed to take only bedding, linen, toilet articles, clothes, kitchen utensils and whatever personal effects they could carry, they were forced to sell their houses, businesses and belongings for a fraction of their worth. They found themselves in the middle of deserts where they broiled in the summer and froze in the winter.

Besides the obvious cruelties, there were more subtle, psychological ones. In the Japanese culture face is all-important, and shame is used to control behavior. Imprisonment was a terrible psychological blow. Janice Mirikitani captures the pain, terror and despair, and courage of that time, in her "Desert Flowers."

In addition, Yoshiko Uchida has written about the proud survivors in her many novels and Jeanne Wakatsuki Houston has won numerous accolades for her *A Farewell to Manzanar*. And her "A Taste of Snow" is a moving testimony to the resilience of the human spirit even in the midst of the suffering.

Many Japanese American boys tried to demonstrate their loyalty to the United States by joining the American Army. A number of them were formed into the 442nd Regimental Combat Team, which lived up to its motto, "Go for broke," in some of the most savage fighting in Europe. In their efforts to prove themselves loyal, they became the most decorated army unit of the war and sustained one of the highest casualty rates. The horrors of such fighting might take years to manifest themselves.

Lane Nishikawa's "They Was Close, Those Brothers" describes one such veteran.

RICHARD HARATANI is a Japanese American who not only writes stories and plays but also acts.

ATTENTION TO DETAIL

Peter Makota knelt over his work, knees padded by a folded towel, eyes intent upon the movement of his brush. With each deft stroke the dark leather shone with added lustre, the polished grain producing a deeper glow. To his left, twelve identical pairs of navy dress shoes sat in scuffed, dull and dusty order, lined in precise rows as if still attached to their officers standing at parade rest. To his right, twenty pair gleamed and glistened, each individual shoe immaculate down to its positioned laces.

Resembling large, shiny beetles, the polished shoes seemed to transcend their surroundings. Shimmering brightly on the bare hardwood floor of the sparsely furnished room, their gleam diminished the effect of the mid-morning sunlight that settled through the single small window, past the tattered curtain tied neatly to the side. The light fell onto a grey metal cot and warmed the coarse grey blanket that lay on top of the worn, thin mattress. Peter kept his shoe wax and polish there while he worked. The two round tins sat on a square of newspaper, sun softened and within easy reach.

Satisfied with the gloss on the shoe in hand, Peter skillfully re-laced it and carefully placed it down so that it began a new row behind the other finished shoes. He picked up the next shoe and began working it with an old toothbrush, dislodging the dirt and debris wedged into its seams and hidden surfaces. As he worked, Peter listened to the familiar movements overhead his basement room; the relaxed sounds of the naval officers enjoying a leisurely Sunday morning in their dining and lounge area.

Many of the officers had been up late the night before in the officers' bar, enjoying the holiday spirits of early winter. Peter had been kept up, busily assisting the bartender and running errands back and forth to the kitchen upstairs. Though it wasn't specifically among his duties as houseboy, Peter helped at the bar most nights since it was next to his quarters and the noise would keep him from sleeping anyway. Sometimes he would be given tips, if the officers had dates whom they wished to impress, and the bar usually closed by one o'clock in the morning so that Peter could be in his bed by two at the latest.

The downstairs area was quiet and desolate on Sunday mornings. Peter had already cleaned up what had been left undone from the night before. He looked forward to finishing with the shoes and being able to enjoy his afternoon off. He planned to catch the twelve-o'clock jitney from the base into town, where his sister Miye worked for a wealthy family. Miye was given the whole day off and they would meet for a walk and sometimes go to see a movie.

A few weekends earlier, no one except Miye was at the house, so she and Peter had sat in the garden and talked. Miye had been very concerned about the war news and she insisted that they both plan to meet, should trouble arise, so they could travel together to their parents' farm in the Central Valley. The war in Europe was worsening and Japan was becoming more and more threatening in the Pacific. Both Peter and Miye felt the growing sense of ill-feeling from those around them, and though Miye continued to go to school, Peter had stopped attending his classes because he felt so alienated.

"I wish I looked like everyone else," Miye had told Peter that day in the garden. He had laughed and admonished her for her silliness, though he had felt the same desire within himself. All their lives they had been prompted by their parents to assimilate into the surrounding culture. They adapted well, but despite their western mannerisms, they were judged first by their appearance. After too many confrontations at school forced Peter to leave, he had found this job, which, if anything, was worse. There were times when he wished that he could shrink into the walls of the officers' club as racial epithets and whiskey-brazened statements were tossed freely about, oblivious of the quiet young man in starched cloth serving drinks and snacks. Sometimes Peter became the target of some demeaning action, but it was seldom intended maliciously, for he was, after all, their houseboy. More often it would be off-hand remarks or thoughtless pranks with Peter as the grinning patsy. Peter was glad that the perpetrators only read his smile and not his eyes.

Some officers disapproved of the treatment Peter was given, but they were not inclined to risk their good standing by defending a subordinate. Peter kept quiet, performed his duties and saved his money towards the day when he could move away and continue his education. He did his job well, taking pride in the quality of his work.

"No matter how small a job may be," his parents had often told him, "it is how you do it that matters."

The shoe was clean. Peter dabbed his cloth into the polish and began touching up the scuff marks, allowing his thoughts to travel freely. His hand motion became automatic as his mind fled to cool hillside creeks where he had stalked native trout as a child.

He could hear the gurgling, melodic water, feel and smell the tree-sweetened breeze. . . . A terse voice snapped out from above and Peter's attention refocused. He listened. There was only the bare sound of a voice crackling from the radio speaker. Peter strained to hear as his hand continued to work the leather. Someone turned up the radio volume, but Peter still could not hear what was being said. Then the upper rooms erupted into a frenzy of shouting, cursing and movement that sent the entire building into a quaking, reverberating motion. Whatever had happened, Peter felt sure that it was something he had better be wary of. There was anger upstairs, and Peter knew that his position lent itself as a convenient vent for anger.

People were running in and out of the building, and from his ground level window Peter saw a flurry of shoes and trousers as the officers hurried about. Jeeps were started up and their tires spun gravel against the building and window glass as they roared off on frantic missions. Peter stood, waiting with apprehension, wondering what to do. His heart went heavy as he heard quick footsteps coming down the wooden steps to the basement. His hand went dead still against the shoe that he held.

A quick rap came loud and sudden against the door, startling Peter in spite of his expectation of it.

"Pee-Wee, you in there?" The voice was Ensign Shepard's.

"Yes sir." Peter was relieved that it was someone friendly, and he turned towards the door as it swung open. The ensign was slightly taller than Peter and about the same age. He looked at Peter, who still held the shoe and dark stained cloth, and the ensign's face was all Peter needed to see.

The ensign explained what had happened at Pearl Harbor while Peter stood silent with disbelief. Peter thought of Miye, and of his parents, and of home. He looked at the ensign and then down at the row of unfinished shoes.

"May I finish these?" he asked. The ensign looked surprised.

"Sure, Pee-Wee, but I don't know if you want to stick around much longer."

Peter nodded.

"I had planned to take the jitney to town at noon."

"I doubt you'd want to do that now." The ensign was pensive. "Look, you go ahead and finish these up and I'll see what I can do about getting you out of here." He looked at Peter with concern. "Say, Pee-Wee, I'd pull that curtain closed and maybe lock the door like you weren't home." He gave Peter a solemn look and then backed out quietly, closing the door as he left.

Peter put the shoe and cloth down and stepped up onto the cot to untie the cord holding the curtain. He drew the cloth along the bent and rusted curtain rod, muting the light in the room. The sunlight coming through the doubled-over cloth created moiré patterns that undulated like wind-swept water against the windowpane. Peter had never noticed the effect before and watched, entranced, while the officers continued passing back and forth beyond the glass. He wondered what would happen now.

Peter stepped down onto the floor and knelt onto the folded towel. He wrapped the shoe that he had been working on in the darkened cloth and with both hands picked it up as if in a private ceremony. He held the shoe with its toe pressed lightly against his abdomen and sat back onto his heels, meditating over the object in his hand. Emotions welled up inside of him and he let them course through his body. Then he breathed deeply and began working on the shoe.

JANICE MIRIKITANI *was sent with other Japanese Americans to the relocation camp at Rohwer.*

DESERT FLOWERS

Flowers
faded
in the desert wind.
No flowers grow
where dust winds blow
and rain is like
a dry heave moan.

Mama, did you dream about that
beau who would take you
away from it all,
who would show you
in his '41 ford
and tell you how soft
your hands
like the silk kimono
you folded for the wedding?
Make you forget
about That place,
the back bending
wind that fell like a wall,
drowned all your geraniums

126

and flooded the shed
where you tried to sleep
away hyenas?
And mama,
bending in the candlelight,
after lights out in barracks,
an ageless shadow
grows victory flowers
made from crepe paper,
shaping those petals
like the tears
your eyes bled.
Your fingers
knotted at knuckles
wounded, winding around wire stems
the tiny, sloganed banner:

"america for americans".

Did you dream
of the shiny ford
(only always a dream)
ride your youth
like the wind
in the headless night?

Flowers
2¢ a dozen,
flowers for American Legions
worn like a badge
on america's lapel

made in post-concentration camps
by candlelight.
Flowers
watered
by the spit
of "no japs wanted here"
planted in poverty
of postwar relocations,
plucked by
victory's veterans.

Mama, do you dream
of the wall of wind
that falls
on your limbless desert,
on stems
brimming with petals/crushed
crepe paper
growing
from the crippled
mouth of your hand?

Your tears, mama,
have nourished us.
Your children
like pollen
scatter in the wind.

JEANNE WAKATSUKI HOUSTON is a Japanese American who lives in Santa Cruz.

A TASTE OF SNOW

I first saw snow one Christmas when I lived in the high desert of Owens Valley, California. I was nine years old. It was during the Second World War, the first winter my family and I spent at Manzanar. When the crystal flakes floated down, like translucent coconut chips dancing in the breeze, I ran out into the clear area between the barracks, twirling and dancing and opening my mouth to catch the powdery ice. The snow reminded me of cotton candy, wispy and delicate, and gone with one whisk of the tongue.

I was surprised by the sharp coldness of the air and somehow disappointed that such beauty had its price to be paid—icy feet and hands, and uncomfortable wetness when the snow melted upon contact with my clothes and face. Still, the utter loveliness of this new phenomenon was so overpowering I soon forgot my discomfort.

Other people began coming out of the barracks into a transformed world. Some carried brightly colored Japanese parasols and wore high wooden *getas* to raise their stockinged feet above the snow. It was odd not to hear the "kata-kata" clatter of wooden clogs scraping across sand and gravel. The blanket of snow muffled sound and thickened the thin planed roofs of the barracks, softening the stark landscape of white on white. It was strangely soothing to me, silent and tranquil. I found myself moved to tears.

This particular imprint in my memory is easily explained. Before being sent to Manzanar we lived in Ocean Park, on Dudley Avenue, a block from the beach. Ocean Park Pier was my playground. All the kids in the neighborhood played ball and skated along the wide cement promenade that bordered the beach from Ocean Park to Venice.

Memories of Ocean Park are warm ones of sunshine, hot days on the beach, building sand castles, playing *Tarzan* and *Jungle Girl*, jumping off lifeguard stands and spraining ankles. Fourth of July was a balmy evening of crowds milling around the pier waiting for fireworks to spray the sky with luminous explosives. Easter was as colorful as the many-hued eggs the local service club buried in the sand for the kids to uncover. And Christmas was just another version of this type of buoyant, high-spirited celebration my family enjoyed before the war.

In my memory Christmas morning seemed always sunny and clear. Strolling along the promenade in my new orange-flowered dress and white high-topped shoes, pushing the doll carriage Santa had left under the big tree in our living room, I proudly displayed myself and my gifts as did the other children of the neighborhood. My oldest brother Bill, who was then in his twenties, walked with me and helped me feed popcorn to the pigeons warbling and pecking around our feet. Then he rushed me off in his old blue roadster to visit his girl friend Molly who played the violin while he sang, and I slept.

Like a story within a story, or a memory within a memory, I cannot think of one memorable Christmas, but of these two. They are yin and yang, each necessary to appreciate the other. I don't remember Christmas trees in Manzanar. But we gathered driftwood from the creeks that poured down from the nearby Sierras and across the high desert. With these we improvised. In my mind's eye they co-exist: a lush, brilliantly lit fir tree; and a bare manzanita limb embellished with origami cranes.

To this day, when I travel in the high country, I can cry seeing nature's exquisite winter garb and remembering my first taste of snow.

—1983

The following is an excerpt from LANE NISHIKAWA's *one-man show,* Life in the Fast Lane. *It is performed without an intermission. Lane is a Japanese American man, about thirty, and is a Sansei.*

   The Punchbowl is a military cemetery in Hawaii. A bento is a kind of Japanese lunch made up of an assortment of foods.

THEY WAS CLOSE, THOSE BROTHERS

Lights up. Lane answers an unseen interviewer.

LANE: Personal stuff? (*Beat*) Well, sure. But it's kind of hard. . . . I mean, because like, it cuts you open and then your insides are all hanging out. . . . Are you for real? . . . Okay, I'll tell ya, sometimes you can get it out and sometimes you just can't. Like I had this Uncle who I was always trying to write about. And, ah, he was my favorite Uncle. My father's brother. His nickname was Blackie. (*Laughs to himself.*) I think everybody from Hawaii has got an Uncle named Blackie. (*Notices she doesn't get it.*) Well, he was the Uncle who gave you a beer when you were eight years old. Or he'd put you on his lap and let you steer the car . . . and he used to play the piano, boogie-woogie type stuff, and the ukulele, and he was always laughing and drinking and having a good time. He was great . . . and you know he fought over in Germany during World War II with the 442nd . . . and he was one of the few guys who survived it all . . . and he brought back his buddies and buried them over at Punchbowl Cemetery . . . in Honolulu. . . . Then after the war, he got married, and had a couple of kids. His wife, my Auntie Jean, was always the nicest to me. He used to be a newswriter for the Honolulu *Star Bulletin* . . . and then well, you see he became a cook, opened up his own okazuya, that's like a family type joint, like a restaurant. . . . I used to go and sit and watch him cook and he'd be kidding me all the time and after work, he'd take me wherever I wanted to go . . . But you see, what I didn't know what that he was having a hard time coping, with all the memories . . . You see, I didn't know that he drank all the time to keep the pain in. . . . Then one day, I find out that my old man is flying back to Hawaii and I know something's wrong. . . . You see, my Uncle Blackie took his own life, and they found him lying on the ground, over at Punchbowl . . . right next to his friends. . . . So man, how do you write about something like that, huh? . . . How do you write about someone that you grew up with and spent half your life . . . about someone who would do

anything for you . . . and you know you gonna
miss . . . about someone who you just loved
with all of your heart . . . about someone who
was so close to you. . . .

Lights slowly fade to black.

*Lane crosses to center stage. We hear birds, tropical, softly
fade in and out as the lights come up.*

*The lights fade up and should be warm, red, orange, and some
blues. We're in Hawaii.*

I flew into Hilo
one August
humid and green
the water aquamarine
boats bumping the harbor
the fish auction
full of a hundred fifty pound ahi
small children
pick up the guts
and leftover cuts
for bait
palm trees
dancing to warm breezes
of island air.

Hilo
on the only island
that still erupts
lava fields

black and red
black and red
for miles and miles
as Pele
Goddess of Fire
lets her hair down
like rain
flowing volcanic fingers
the size of buildings
the petrified trees
the forgotten forest.

(Uncle Sharkey's voice, heavy Hawaiian accent)
Ay, this is where
your father's home used to be.
Right there
in that park.
You know, when he was one kid
whoa
tidal wave
tore 'em apart.
Ay, you see that.
Way over there.
That's the breakers.
Hilo Bay breakers.
Stop one tidal wave, eh.
Stop the sea.
You know, your father
and your Uncle Blackie
their parents die

when your father
was only five years old.
They was raised
by their Auntie and Uncle, you know.
Yeah
they was close, those brothers.

(*Old woman's voice*)
Kiyoshi.

(*Back to Lane*)
My Great-Aunt
her voice a whisper.
She smiled
and looked up at me.
What did she say?

(*Uncle Sharkey*)
She said you remind her of Kiyoshi.
Uncle Blackie.
Your face.
Yeah, you.

(*Lane*)
closed my eyes
and we thumbed through albums
pictures from the past.
My Oji-chan
in a kimono
Nishikawa family
Hiroshima-ken

a young man
about to leave
his family behind.
My Oba-chan
so beautiful
her face
calm.

(*Uncle Sharkey*)
They died so young though.
Your Oba-chan was first.
She was very sick, you know.
Then your Oji-chan follow her.
His grief release him, eh.
I think so.
Ay, see your father
and your Uncle Blackie
just boys, eh.

(*Lane*)
Innocent and shy
as I once was.

(*Sharkey*)
You know
those brothers
they love to go surfcast.

(*Lane*)
Yeah, I remember.
They took me many times

at dusk
after work
we'd go out to the beach
cut up some shrimp
cast our lines
poles stuck in the sand
a small bell on each
then the tide
took the bait
out and in
out and in.
We'd sit
talk story
drink beer
bento
laugh
until the moon and the stars
shined down on the ocean
black as the sky.
You're right
they were close, those brothers.

(Sharkey)
  See here
  your Uncle
  military khakis, eh.
  His face, dark.
  His hair, black and shiny.
  1940's style, eh.
  Greased back.

Ay, look at his grin
just like yours.

(*Lane*)
  Yeah
  I can see him
  I can hear him.

Lights slowly shift to eerie blues. We hear Uncle Blackie's voiceover.

  I'm sorry
  but it's the only way
  the only way.

(*Lane*)
  But Uncle
  why'd you do it
  the war was over
  it was in the past
  your wife
  the kids
  what they going do now
  what'd you do something like that for?

For the first three lines Uncle Blackie's voice is heard, Lane will blend in with the voiceover. Uncle Blackie's voice fades out on the word die.

  I'm sorry
  but it's the only way

when you watch
your lifelong friends
die
next to you
slowly
all the way home
and all you can do
is hold them
hoping your warmth
will give them life
but nightmares
they can't be buried
like ashes
they follow you
all the way home.
Life is hard
when you filled with pride
when you love your family
so much
but no education
no chance
no friends
left to be buried
so you drink
until you forget
until all the memories
go out
with the tide
but nightmares
they can't be buried

like ashes
they follow you
all the way home.

But what about me
what about my father?

Lights slowly change back to warms.

Don't worry, eh.
He knows
he understands
he knows.
Ay, my spirit
is in you
you hold 'em now
inside &
carry yourself
as I did
very proud
and don't lose that spirit
cause I had one hard life
to make 'em easy
for you
Kiyoshi
for you.

Fade to black.

Love

In adolescence, the Asian American wanders not only into that part of the Hopescape defined by identity, but also into that very human area called love. The guideposts would be confusing enough even if there were only one set.

In Asia, as in many European countries, marriage was a social rather than an individual decision. Sometimes the parents arranged the marriage so that bride and groom never met until the day of the wedding. However, it was also possible for even well-bred young men and women to catch a glimpse of one another and suggest the match to their parents—though their parents would have the final say. It goes without saying that the prospective marriage partner would be of a respectable family and from the same class.

Sometimes the arranged marriages resulted in tragic mismatches, with little regard paid to the young couple's wishes. Coming to America only exacerbated the differences—as seen in Wakako Yamauchi's poignant "And the Soul Shall Dance"—especially given the rural isolation of so many Asian women.

The conflict between the Old World and the New becomes sharpest when it comes to romance; and many Asian American teenagers find themselves caught between two worlds. Longhang Nguyen expresses that dilemma in her lyrical "Rain Music," in which a young girl is torn between her family's expectations and her own desires.

However, America can produce changes, especially for women. In Julie Yabu's "A Lesson from the Heart," a grandmother and granddaughter go cruising and wind up teaching each other.

WAKAKO YAMAUCHI *was born in the Imperial Valley in California to Japanese American farmers. Her stage adaptation of this story won the Los Angeles Critics' Circle Award in 1977.*

AND THE SOUL SHALL DANCE

I t's all right to talk about it now. Most of the principals are dead, except, of course, me and my younger brother, and possibly Kiyoko Oka, who might be near forty-five now, because, yes, I'm sure of it, she was fourteen then. I was nine, and my brother about four, so he hardly counts at all. Kiyoko's mother is dead, my father is dead, my mother is dead, and her father could not have lasted all these years with his tremendous appetite for alcohol and pickled chilies—those little yellow ones, so hot they could make your mouth hurt; he'd eat them like peanuts and tears would surge from his bulging thyroid eyes in great waves and stream down the dark coarse terrain of his face.

My father farmed then in the desert basin resolutely named Imperial Valley, in the township called Westmoreland; twenty acres of tomatoes, ten of summer squash, or vice versa, and the Okas lived maybe a mile, mile and a half, across an alkaline road, a stretch of greasewood, tumbleweed, and white sand, to the south of us. We didn't hobnob much with them, because you see, they were a childless couple and we were a family: father, mother, daughter, and son, and we went to the Buddhist church on Sundays where my mother taught Japanese, and the Okas kept pretty much to themselves. I don't mean they were unfriendly; Mr. Oka would sometimes walk over (he rarely drove) on rainy days, all dripping wet, short and squat under a soggy newspaper, pretending to need a plow-blade or a file, and he would spend the afternoon in our kitchen drinking sake and eating chilies with my father. As he got progressively drunker, his large mouth would draw down and with the stream of tears, he looked like a kindly weeping bullfrog.

Not only were they childless, impractical in an area where large families were looked upon as labor potentials, but there was a certain strangeness about them. I became aware of it the summer our bathhouse burned down, and my father didn't get right down to building another, and a Japanese without a bathhouse . . . well, Mr. Oka offered us the use of his. So every night that summer we drove to the Okas for our bath, and we came in frequent contact with Mrs. Oka, and this is where I found the strangeness.

Mrs. Oka was small and spare. Her clothes hung on her like loose skin and when she walked, the skirt about her legs gave her a sort of webbed look. She was pretty in spite of the boniness and the dull calico and the barren look; I know now she couldn't have been over thirty. Her eyes were large and a little vacant, although once I saw them fill with tears; the time I insisted we take the old Victrola over and we played our Japanese records for her. Some of the songs were sad, and I imagined the nostalgia she felt, but my mother said the tears were probably from yawning or from the smoke of her cigarettes. I thought my mother resented her for not being more hospitable; indeed, never a cup of tea appeared before us, and between them the conversation of women was totally absent: the rise and fall of gentle voices, the arched eyebrows, the croon of polite surprise. But more than this, Mrs. Oka was *different*.

Obviously she was shy, but some nights she disappeared altogether. She would see us drive into her yard and then lurch from sight. She was gone all evening. Where could she have hidden in that two-roomed house—where in that silent desert? Some nights she would wait out our visit with enormous forbearance, quietly pushing wisps of stray hair behind her ears and waving gnats away from her great moist eyes, and some nights she moved about with nervous agitation, her khaki canvas shoes slapping loudly as she walked. And sometimes there appeared to be welts and bruises on her usually smooth brown face, and she would sit solemnly, hands on lap, eyes large and intent on us. My mother hurried us home then: "Hurry, Masako, no need to wash well; hurry."

You see, being so poky, I was always last to bathe. I think the Okas bathed after we left because my mother often reminded me to keep the water clean. The routine was to lather outside the tub (there were buckets and pans and a small wooden stool), rinse off the soil and soap, and then soak in the tub of hot hot water and contemplate. Rivulets of perspiration would run down the scalp.

When my mother pushed me like this, I dispensed

with ritual, rushed a bar of soap around me and splashed
about a pan of water. So hastily toweled, my wet skin
trapped the clothes to me, impeding my already clumsy
progress. Outside, my mother would be murmuring her
many apologies and my father, I knew, would be carrying
my brother whose feet were already sandy. We would
hurry home.

I thought Mrs. Oka might be insane and I asked my
mother about it, but she shook her head and smiled with
her mouth drawn down and said that Mrs. Oka loved
her sake. This was unusual, yes, but there were other unusual women we knew. Mrs. Nagai was bought by her
husband from a geisha house; Mrs. Tani was a militant
Christian Scientist; Mrs. Abe, the midwife, was occult.
My mother's statement explained much: sometimes Mrs.
Oka was drunk and sometimes not. Her taste for liquor
and cigarettes was a step in the realm of men; unusual for
a Japanese wife, but at that time, in that place, and to
me, Mrs. Oka loved her sake in the way my father loved
his, in the way of Mr. Oka, the way I loved my candy.
That her psychology may have demanded this anesthetic,
that she lived with something unendurable, did not occur
to me. Nor did I perceive the violence of emotions that
the purple welts indicated—or the masochism that per-
mitted her to display these wounds to us.

In spite of her masculine habits, Mrs. Oka was never
less than a woman. She was no lady in the area of social
amenities; but the feminine in her was innate and never
left her. Even in her disgrace, she was a small broken
sparrow, slightly floppy, too slowly enunciating her few

words, too carefully rolling her Bull Durham, cocking her small head and moistening the ocher tissue. Her aberration was a protest of the life assigned her; it was obstinate, but unobserved, alas, unheeded. "Strange" was the only concession we granted her.

Toward the end of summer, my mother said we couldn't continue bathing at the Okas'; when winter set in we'd all catch our death from the commuting and she'd always felt dreadful about our imposition on Mrs. Oka. So my father took the corrugated tin sheets he'd found on the highway and had been saving for some other use and built up our bathhouse again. Mr. Oka came to help.

While they raised the quivering tin walls, Mr. Oka began to talk. His voice was sharp and clear above the low thunder of the metal sheets.

He told my father he had been married in Japan previously to the present Mrs. Oka's older sister. He had a child by the marriage, Kiyoko, a girl. He had left the two to come to America intending to send for them soon, but shortly after his departure, his wife passed away from an obscure stomach ailment. At the time, the present Mrs. Oka was young and had foolishly become involved with a man of poor reputation. The family was anxious to part the lovers and conveniently arranged a marriage by proxy and sent him his dead wife's sister. Well that was all right, after all, they were kin, and it would be good for the child when she came to join them. But things didn't work out that way; year after year he postponed calling for his daughter, couldn't get the price of fare together, and the wife—ahhh, the wife, Mr. Oka's groan was lost in the rumble of his hammering.

He cleared his throat. The girl was now fourteen, he said, and begged to come to America to be with her own real family. Those relatives had forgotten the favor he'd done in accepting a slightly used bride, and now tormented his daughter for being forsaken. True, he'd not sent much money, but if they knew, if they only knew how it was here.

"Well," he sighed, "who could be blamed? It's only right she be with me anyway."

"That's right," my father said.

"Well, I sold the horse and some other things and managed to buy a third-class ticket on the Taiyo-Maru. Kiyoko will get here the first week of September." Mr. Oka glanced toward my father, but my father was peering into a bag of nails. "I'd be much obliged to you if your wife and little girl," he rolled his eyes toward me, "would take kindly to her. She'll be lonely."

Kiyoko-san came in September. I was surprised to see so very nearly a woman; short, robust, buxom: the female counterpart of her father; thyroid eyes and protruding teeth, straight black hair banded impudently into two bristly shucks, Cuban heels and white socks. Mr. Oka brought her proudly to us.

"Little Masako here," for the first time to my recollection, he touched me; he put his rough fat hand on the top of my head, "is very smart in school. She will help you with your school work, Kiyoko," he said.

I had so looked forward to Kiyoko-san's arrival. She

would be my soul mate; in my mind I had conjured a girl of my own proportions: thin and tall, but with the refinement and beauty I didn't yet possess that would surely someday come to the fore. My disappointment was keen and apparent. Kiyoko-san stepped forward shyly, then retreated with a short bow and small giggle, her fingers pressed to her mouth.

My mother took her away. They talked for a long time—about Japan, about enrollment in American school, the clothes Kiyoko-san would need, and where to look for the best values. As I watched them, it occurred to me that I had been deceived: this was not a child, this was a woman. The smile pressed behind her fingers, the way of her nod, so brief, like my mother when father scolded her: the face was inscrutable, but something— maybe spirit—shrank visibly, like a piece of silk in water. I was disappointed; Kiyoko-san's soul was barricaded in her unenchanting appearance and the smile she fenced behind her fingers. She started school from third grade, one below me, and as it turned out, she quickly passed me by. There wasn't much I could help her with except to drill her on pronunciation—the "L" and "R" sounds. Every morning walking to our rural school: land, leg, library, loan, lot; every afternoon returning home: ran, rabbit, rim, rinse, roll. That was the extent of our communication; friendly but uninteresting.

One particularly cold November night—the wind outside was icy; I was sitting on my bed, my brother's and mine, oiling the cracks in my chapped hands by lamplight—someone rapped urgently at our door. It was

Kiyoko-san; she was hysterical, she wore no wrap, her teeth were chattering, and except for the thin straw zori, her feet were bare. My mother led her to the kitchen, started a pot of tea, and gestured to my brother and me to retire. I lay very still but because of my brother's restless tossing and my father's snoring, was unable to hear much. I was aware, though, that drunken and savage brawling had brought Kiyoko-san to us. Presently they came to the bedroom. I feigned sleep. My mother gave Kiyoko-san a gown and pushed me over to make room for her. My mother spoke firmly: "Tomorrow you will return to them; you must not leave them again. They are your people." I could almost feel Kiyoko-san's short nod.

All night long I lay cramped and still, afraid to intrude into her hulking back. Two or three times her icy feet jabbed into mine and quickly retreated. In the morning I found my mother's gown neatly folded on the spare pillow. Kiyoko-san's place in bed was cold.

She never came to weep at our house again but I know she cried: her eyes were often swollen and red. She stopped much of her giggling and routinely pressed her fingers to her mouth. Our daily pronunciation drill petered off from lack of interest. She walked silently with her shoulders hunched, grasping her books with both arms, and when I spoke to her in my halting Japanese, she absently corrected my prepositions.

Spring comes early in the Valley; in February the skies are clear though the air is still cold. By March, winds are vigorous and warm and wild flowers dot the desert floor, cockleburs are green and not yet tenacious, the sand is crusty underfoot, everywhere there is the smell of things growing and the first tomatoes are showing green and bald.

As the weather changed, Kiyoko-san became noticeably more cheerful. Mr. Oka who hated so to drive could often be seen steering his dusty old Ford over the road that passes our house, and Kiyoko-san sitting in front would sometimes wave gaily to us. Mrs. Oka was never with them. I thought of these trips as the westernizing of Kiyoko-san: with a permanent wave, her straight black hair became tangles of tiny frantic curls; between her textbooks she carried copies of *Modern Screen* and *Photoplay*, her clothes were gay with print and piping, and she bought a pair of brown suede shoes with alligator trim. I can see her now picking her way gingerly over the deceptive white peaks of alkaline crust. At first my mother watched their coming and going with vicarious pleasure. "Probably off to a picture show; the stores are all closed at this hour," she might say. Later her eyes would get distant and she would muse, "They've left her home again; Mrs. Oka is alone again, the poor woman."

Now when Kiyoko-san passed by or came in with me on her way home, my mother would ask about Mrs. Oka—how is she, how does she occupy herself these rainy days, or these windy or warm or cool days. Often the answers were polite: "Thank you, we are fine," but sometimes Kiyoko-san's upper lip would pull over her teeth, and her voice would become very soft and she would say, "Drink, always drinking and fighting." At those times my mother would invariably say, "Endure, soon you will be marrying and going away."

Once a young truck driver delivered crates at the Oka farm and he dropped back to our place to tell my father that Mrs. Oka had lurched behind his truck while he was backing up, and very nearly let him kill her. Only the daughter pulling her away saved her, he said. Thoroughly unnerved, he stopped by to rest himself and talk about it. Never, never, he said in wide-eyed wonder, had he seen a drunken Japanese woman. My father nodded gravely, "Yes, it's unusual," he said and drummed his knee with his fingers.

Evenings were longer now, and when my mother's migraines drove me from the house in unbearable self-pity, I would take walks in the desert. One night with the warm wind against me, the dune primrose and yellow poppies closed and fluttering, the greasewood swaying in languid orbit, I lay on the white sand beneath a shrub and tried to disappear.

A voice sweet and clear cut through the half-dark of the evening:

> Red lips press against a glass
> Drink the purple wine
> And the soul shall dance

Mrs. Oka appeared to be gathering flowers. Bending, plucking, standing, searching, she added to a small bouquet she clasped. She held them away; looked at them slyly, lids lowered, demure, then in a sudden and sinuous movement, she broke into a stately dance. She stopped, gathered more flowers, and breathed deeply into them.

Tossing her head, she laughed—softly, beautifully, from her dark throat. The picture of her imagined grandeur was lost to me, but the delusion that transformed the bouquet of tattered petals and sandy leaves, and the aloneness of a desert twilight into a fantasy that brought such joy and abandon made me stir with discomfort. The sound broke Mrs. Oka's dance. Her eyes grew large and her neck tense—like a cat on the prowl. She spied me in the bushes. A peculiar chill ran through me. Then abruptly and with childlike delight, she scattered the flowers around her and walked away singing:

Falling, falling, petals on a wind . . .

That was the last time I saw Mrs. Oka. She died before the spring harvest. It was pneumonia. I didn't attend the funeral, but my mother said it was sad. Mrs. Oka looked peaceful, and the minister expressed the irony of the long separation of Mother and Child and the short-lived re-union; hardly a year together, she said. We went to help Kiyoko-san address and stamp those black-bordered acknowledgements.

When harvest was over, Mr. Oka and Kiyoko-san moved out of the Valley. We never heard from them or saw them again and I suppose in a large city, Mr. Oka found some sort of work, perhaps as a janitor or a dishwasher and Kiyoko-san grew up and found someone to marry.

LONGHANG NGUYEN *is a Vietnamese American writer who immigrated to the United States in 1979 and has settled in California.*

RAIN MUSIC

Linh and I grew up penned in the same yard, so our sibling rivalry did not last very long. By third grade we had stopped physically assaulting one another and reached a permanent truce. At that time her hair was long and flowing, brushed daily by my mother as Linh closed her eyes and counted each stroke. It always felt like cool satin when I yanked it, her head jerking backward, mimicking the motion of my arm. In actuality, she was very kind and I was not too violent, so we became intimate friends. I have not had any trouble from her since.

She is the red rose of the family and I am the green thorn. We have both decided that we are beautiful, so she tells me, but I believe she is also very beautiful outside in face and gesture. I always pout when I accuse her of being a selfish firstborn, picking, stealing the best of our parents' genes and leaving me the rejected remainder. She has wide, almond-shaped eyes like black, pearl-black reflecting pools with brown-colored flecks swirling beneath the surface, light honey-color skin and even, velvet-smooth cheeks. Her nose is just slightly upturned, her lips rosebud shaped, her chin small and delicate. Her hair still looks and feels the same now as in third grade. The vision, taken together as a whole, is breathtaking. There is something about it, a wistful, dandelion, orchid-like kind of beauty that feels like notes in a chord being played separately, finger by finger, harmonizing back and forth. I marvel even now.

My mother and father have polished her until she shines. She graduated summa cum laude from the College of Chemistry at Cal and double majored in Ethnic Studies. However, my parents don't count the latter. She is now a fourth-year student at UCSF preparing to enter the surgical residency program next fall. My parents are bursting at the seams, gorged with devouring so much blessedness and good fortune.

"Will your daughter become a surgeon?" our relatives ask.

"It's possible," my father says, beaming.

"She is friends with this young man in her class. He's tall, distinguished-looking, loyal and respectful to his parents, hard-working but generous. He was even born in Vietnam! But he came over here with his family in 1975. He went to Harvard"—my mother pauses to let the relatives gasp in unison—"on a full scholarship!" She smiles modestly, then lowers her eyes.

"A possible son-in-law?" they ask.

She shrugs and sighs. "That is up to God."

Linh hasn't told my parents about David. She met him five years ago during her final year at Cal. That semester they were in three classes together: a choral class, an Afro-American literature class, and a creative writing class. They became good friends.

David is a writer. His subjects are ordinary preoccupations of other writers: his mother, the father he has never seen or known, the friends of his childhood. Some of them are dead now. The others are spread out across the country. One is a construction worker in St. Louis. Another is a teacher in Baton Rouge. The third is a journalist in Washington, D.C. They write to him once in a while or call him. Linh hasn't met any of them, but she knows them all.

After David feverishly completes a story, Linh cooks him dinner. Afterward, she tucks him into bed and sits nearby in the wicker chair, legs drawn up and hugged tightly to her chest, to watch him while he sleeps. His soft, black curls rest against the white of the pillow, his closed eyelids and long lashes flutter minutely while he dreams, his breath whistles through the evenness of his teeth as the cover grazes the dark honey of his skin.

They always have a good time together, and he makes her laugh in many different ways, wherever they happen to be. He always gets close to finishing her off during a tennis set, but then she cries out that he has cheated and treated her unfairly and he has to start over again. He never wins. Sometimes they sing together, his clear, resonant tenor melding with her flutelike, crystalline soprano. Then they have tea.

I know all about David. She won't stop talking about him, but I know less about Thanh, the Vietnamese friend at UCSF. I know he's nice but that's all. She woke me up this morning at ten thirty and said, "It's a bright, beautiful, Saturday morning. Let's go and have a picnic."

"No, no," I mumbled hazily in my sleep. "Take David. Leave me alone."

"I don't want to take David. I want to spend quality time with you, my darling sister. Get up, you piece of mutton. Toast on the table in five minutes and we're leaving in half an hour."

"Oh, lord," I groaned, "I'm being punished for sins from past lives."

We arrived at the park at twelve, lugged our ample picnic hamper heavily laden with cheese, fruits, sandwiches, ice, and bottles of juice from the car, and trudged into the heart of the lightly shaded, green forest. When I opened the basket and took out the butter, she started to talk.

"David kissed me last night . . ."

"He what?"

". . . or I kissed him. It just happened, I guess. He invited me to dinner, promised to cook a sumptuous Cajun feast with Vietnamese desserts. *Bánh flanc*, you know. My favorite." She plucked a blade of grass from its roots and twisted it back and forth, watching a streak of feeble, yellow sun play on its linear edges. "I expected it to be a celebration. He'd just finished his first novel, not quite a love story, he says, and he wanted me to read it." She spoke more softly. "When I arrived, he had set tiny blossoms in water dishes throughout the apartment. It smelled wonderful. The food was delicious, everything so lovely, so tranquil I didn't know where to begin. After dinner he led me into the living room.

"'Rain music,' he said. 'It's for you.' After the last note

on the piano had stopped to echo, he turned toward me and kissed me for a long, long time. I didn't know what I was doing. I just couldn't stop. I didn't breathe. When he let me go, I kept thinking of his hands and fingers, seeing them fly over the ivory keys like little Russian men dancing in their black fur hats and noticing how his brown was different from mine. I was raging inside, screaming in my head, 'Why can't his fingers be brown like mine, be my brown? Why is his hair curly, not straight like mine?' I saw brown pigments run across my eyes, all different colored browns. Those pigments keep us apart. How do I stand there and tell this man who writes me music and whose hands burn my cheeks that I can't be who he wants me to be?"

"But he doesn't want to change you."

"No, I can't be who he thinks I am. He's a damned starving writer. He can't give me anything, just himself. And he doesn't even know that I'm using him. Damn it! He doesn't even know." She choked on her tears, swallowed, and cried quietly, hugging her knees, until exhausted. The leaves rustled softly while I waited.

After a while she grew calm, her eyes gazing steadily at the flashing water of the stream below. "I love Thanh. I would never hurt him for anything. Throughout the four years at UCSF, he has been so patient, so kind, so dedicated to medicine for its own good, not for just its technology, even though he's brilliant and understands these details completely. He's so perfect for me, just perfect. It's like he stepped out of my story and came to life. We speak the same language and share the same past. Everything. And Mom and Dad, they've done so much for us. Now they think they've won the lottery from God for being good all their life."

"But how do you feel about Thanh? How does he make you feel?"

"He will be my lifelong friend. He'll make a wonderful father. That's what a husband should be. Our children will know the culture and customs of our homeland. They'll speak Vietnamese and English, just like us."

"And how does David make you feel?" I tugged at her gently.

She bowed her head for a long while reflecting. Then she softly murmured, "It's just not possible."

"But why? I don't understand."

The picnic basket remained quite full. Neither of us was hungry. It threatened to rain as we packed up to go home. On the drive back, we were silent. I watched the windshield wipers swing back and forth, clearing rain cascading down the front window.

JULIE YABU is a Japanese-Korean American who manages to find the time to write fiction in the midst of her medical studies at Baylor College of Medicine.

A LESSON FROM THE HEART

"Y ou've grown so much . . . and it's time you met a man," my grandmother said, scrutinizing me through her round, thick bifocals. "A good man. No, the best man." She pinched my left cheek until she left a red mark.

"It's okay, Hamai," I said, looking down at my watch and biting my lower lip until it bled. Hamai was what we called her in Korean.

She was wearing her usual outfit for public appearance—a color-coordinated pants suit. Her polyester, elasticized-waist pants with wide legs discreetly covered the brace on her left leg, and the matching jacket hid her hunched back.

"You know, I used to have hundreds of men lined up at my door and calling me every night to ask me out. All the other girls looked at me with envy. Don't think that I don't know how to catch a man," she snapped. Her voice acquired a sharper, defensive tone as she firmly pulled down the sides of her jacket, which reached just past her hips.

"I thought you wanted help shopping for groceries," I protested.

161

However, Hamai had already made up her mind. "I'm going to teach you how to catch the 'right' man."

I was stuck. Hamai always got her way, and no one dared to go against her wishes.

Of course, we went to her favorite place, a small park about two blocks from her apartment. She insisted that we walk despite the doctor's warnings against it—and despite the fact that she had just recovered from a stroke. I walked slowly by her side, allowing her to stump along with the support of her newly finished wooden cane. I smiled to myself, remembering the months that we had spent—even buying the most expensive cane—convincing her that she must use it. "I can walk alone," she would always say.

We sat in her usual spot, an old wooden bench that resembled a rocking chair with two seats. Above us, the same huge oak tree looked down upon us almost as if my grandma had instructed it to protect us. A winding concrete pathway, with lots of cracks where weeds managed to grow, was right in front of us. People occasionally walked this way as a shortcut but were usually in a rush to get to work. Rarely did families come and spend the day here.

We must have looked like an odd couple. My grandma was leaning back with her legs dangling off the bench. Looking at her at that moment, I understood why people always told me that I had a "cute" grandma. Her plump figure, accentuated by the light blue matching outfit, and her short, jet-black, tightly permed hair framing a porcelain-white, perfectly round face, made her resemble an

Asian Mrs. Beasley doll. In contrast, I was sitting Indian style on the bench, wearing old cutoff jeans and a white tank top. My hair was tied back in a loose ponytail with strands falling out around my face, and my golden-brown, sun-baked skin was evidence that I spent most of my summer days in the sun.

After a few minutes a man wearing a three-piece suit and carrying a briefcase walked by. He trudged along and stooped forward a little. I carefully watched my grandma's eyes follow him until he disappeared around the curve of the pathway.

She blinked once very hard and wrinkled her eyebrows, forming a deep crease across her forehead.

After speculating for a moment, she said, "He stoops like a tree—how do you think he can support himself or you?" My grandma was famous for her endless supply of sayings or superstitions.

Then she darted her eyes at me and ordered, "Sit up straight and present yourself like a lady. How do you expect a man to ever look at you when you sit and act like an uncivilized person?"

I sat up straight and watched a meticulously dressed man, wearing pressed white slacks and a matching dress shirt and with almost "plastic" hair, walk by with his head held up high. I merely gazed at him in awe. "That's him, Hamai," I sighed.

She frowned in amazement at my ignorance. "Julie, what's wrong with you? A man like that spends more time looking into a mirror than anything else."

Within the next few hours, more men passed by along

with more criticisms from my grandma. Not one man matched my grandma's strict standards. We waited as the sun slowly faded away and hid itself behind the branches of the tree. Silence overtook us for a few minutes, and I could only hear the wind rustling through the leaves of the tree.

My grandma looked off absently toward where the pathway ended. "This was exactly the type of day that I last saw your grandfather," she murmured. "He was a good man . . . the best I've ever seen. I spent years by the window every morning waiting for him to come back . . . until twenty years later I realized that I wasn't going to see him ever again. Finally, I had to move on and continue alone."

I put my hand sympathetically over hers and let the tips of my fingers run over the calluses and wrinkles that covered her hand. Her hands alone were proof that she had never run away from her hard life.

She covered my hand with her other hand. "I still remember smelling the salty sea air and standing on the boat holding your mother's hand as I watched the last of our country. I was determined to leave my old life and dreams and never go back." The wooden bench began to rock back and forth as if we were on the boat once again.

Suddenly, she squeezed my hand hard. "I wasted so many years expecting him to come back because I was afraid of being alone," she quavered as years of built-up anguish burst out.

I leaned over, put my arm around her shoulder, and gently rubbed the collar of her jacket. "But Hamai, you're never alone. . . . I'll come live with you after I finish school, and we could have our 'secret talks' about men every day," I tried to reassure her.

Hamai didn't respond for a few minutes and instead gently bowed her head and closed her eyes. Suddenly, she looked up at me, clamped a hand on either side of my face, and looked straight at me. "I've already lived for eighty-seven years and had my chance; but you're so young, with all your life ahead of you. More than I ever had. Don't make the same mistakes that I did. Be strong. Be independent." Her voice became very sharp.

I looked into my grandma's eyes, seeing the sparkle and youthfulness between the folds of loose skin and wrinkles. I wrapped my arms around her, rested my head on her shoulder, and smelled the baby powder on her cheek that always made it as soft as kid leather.

Guides

The American Hopescape is ever changing, and the change of pace has accelerated. Lost in that Hopescape and often in conflict with their parents, Asian American teenagers sometimes turn to their grandparents for guidance. As earlier explorers in life if not in the American Hopescape, grandparents can provide at least a sense of direction and perhaps even the directions themselves. In "Yai," Visalaya Hirunpidok's grandmother gives her granddaughter the kind of insight that will serve her well when she returns to America.

Sometimes the help must must come through a series of confrontations, as it does in Ann Tashi Slater's "There's No Reason to Get Romantic." Coming to terms with her grandmother also means coming to terms with her own self.

Of course, there are growing numbers of Asian American children who have been adopted by white families or, as in the case of Amy Ling, are the children of such adopted Asian children. Amy Ling's "Grandmother Traub" is a sensitive portrait of a loving woman and what she gained from her adopted family. But she also demonstrates that it is possible to keep one's Asian roots in "Grandmother Ling."

The bond between grandparent and grandchild can extend even beyond death and can be a special treasure of childhood, as Rebecca Honma shows in "Jijan."

Finally, William Wu's story "Black Powder" reminds us that the Hopescape is not just ever changing. It is self-renewing as the teenagers of today become grandparents themselves; and the questions they ask today will have even more importance in a future time.

VISALAYA HIRUNPIDOK is a Thai American writer who is currently studying at Berkeley.

YAI

The sky appeared still and gray as the plane gradually descended through the dense clouds and lowered its wheels. It had been an exhausting flight, but the Korean Airlines 747 jet was finally making its landing in Bangkok, Thailand.

Though I had been born here, I had left Thailand at the age of two. Ten years later, everything seemed new. The preparations for the trip and the plane ride itself had seemed almost like a dream. Until now, Thailand had only been a place within my imagination.

Eagerly I leaned forward in the narrow aisle and peered out in space between the seat rows, at the tiny window. I had to twist my head at an awkward angle before I saw the greenish brown landscape of Thailand sweep by down below—patches of rice fields and grasses spotted with rickety wooden stilt houses on either side of a sinuously winding, muddy canal.

The seat-belt warning lights blinked to the tone of xylophone bars, the lights within the cabin dimmed, and the pilot's voice droned over the intercom. Between his Korean accent and the muffled tone of the tiny speaker, it was difficult to understand his words. "We are approaching Bangkok. It is now four twenty-four P.M. Our estimated arrival is five P.M," he announced.

Sitting next to my older sister, I braced myself as the plane dove toward Dawn Muang Airport. On the other side, I saw my mother unusually tense. Sitting restlessly on her seat, her fingers fumbled and fidgeted over her seatbelt buckle for an agitated moment. I thought it was the sharp descent that troubled her.

As the heavy steel airplane door opened, I could feel a warm gust of air rush into the chilly air-conditioned compartment of the airplane. I had finally arrived in Thailand. It really existed and I was there.

Lugging our carry-on baggage, my mother, sister, and I made our way down the steel staircase from the plane to a waiting bus ready to shuttle us to the arrival area inside the airport building.

I insisted on carrying the giant stuffed animal I had won from the San Pedro Pier game room and arcade back in California. It was a giant gray hippopotamus half my size, and it had taken twenty dollars' worth of baseballs and a highly refined tossing skill to acquire this prized portly creature.

Although I had wanted to keep it for myself—since it had been the biggest prize I had ever won at a game room—I decided that I had enough creatures at home, and my cousin Owp would enjoy it more. Having ventured this far with this huge, cumbersome animal and its silly grin, I couldn't wait to give it to her and make her happy.

With so many passengers crammed into the crowded

bus, the warm humid air quickly became stifling. After having easily passed through the Thai customs, we picked up our luggage at the baggage claim carousel and exited out the gates. Beyond them a throng of people waited behind a partition. Their loud, excited chatter almost drowned out the distant sound of honking cars and roaring jets. As announcements boomed and echoed from above, I surveyed the crowd for a familiar face. However, the only photographs I had seen had been ten years old and I recognized no one.

A handful of beaming people burst from the crowd toward us. A short, slender woman with pale skin and short black hair patted my shoulder and smiled agreeably.

The woman was introduced as my Aunt Aiw. She was my mother's younger sister, and we were going to be living in her house during our stay in Thailand.

Two small men wearing light cotton short-sleeved shirts joined her. Their rough, tanned, leathery faces gazed admiringly at my sister and me.

Deftly, they swept our bags out of our hands. They would have taken my hippo, too, but I held it securely against me as I met my other relatives. I was finally meeting some of my mother's brothers and sisters, my aunts and uncles.

Carried away by all the excitement and welcomes, I greeted anyone and everyone around me without even knowing their exact relationship to me.

Putting my hippo down momentarily, I pressed my hands together in a gesture Westerners usually associate with prayer and said, "*Sawadee ca.*" I promptly repeated,

"*Sawadee ca.*" It was Thai for "hello" and an acknowledgment of respect for the other person. "*Took kon sabai, mai ca?*" That was the Thai for "Is everyone doing well?"

I wanted to make sure I didn't miss anyone. My mother had trained me to follow this traditional Thai custom while growing up, and I wasn't going to forget it now. When everyone suddenly began to laugh, I became worried that I had done something wrong.

"That's your younger cousin Danai," my aunt said, chuckling. "You don't have to gesture to him, since he's younger than you."

Trying to be agreeable, but still anxious, I just smiled and laughed along with everyone.

Still more relatives waited outside by a caravan of compact diesel cars. "How was the flight? How long has it been since I've seen you? I can't believe how much you children have grown. You've changed so much, Sister, I couldn't even recognize you. What do you think of Thailand these days? How long will you be staying here? We'll have so many places to go to. . . ." Embracing each of us, inundating us with an endless stream of questions, helping us with our luggage and smiling and nodding every which way, everyone seemed to be in a frenzy of excitement and enthusiasm.

I surrendered my hippo to an uncle only grudgingly. After having come so far with it, I was fearful of losing it in the confusion of the moment.

"What is this doll?" he inquired. "Things from America are funny and unusual."

"It's a present for Cousin Owp," I said. "I won it from a

ball-tossing game at San Pedro Pier."

"You must be a clever little girl to have won so big a prize. I'm sure your cousin will like it very much," he said. "I'll take very good care of it for now and place it in the trunk with your baggage."

"Thank you," I said, out of politeness.

The hippo under his big arm wobbled up and down with every brisk step he took. He sprang open the trunk, placed the hippo on the sidewalk, put some luggage flat inside the space, and then gently laid the hippo down atop the luggage, knowing I was watching him every step of the way. With the hippo safely tucked away inside the trunk, he slammed it shut.

As I approached a car with tinted windows, my aunt told me that Grandmother was waiting in it. She was too weak and tired to walk all the way into the crowded airport. As we neared the car, my mother's jubilant flow of conversation stopped.

As she stood before the car door, I could sense my mother once again growing agitated. So it had not been the airplane's descent that had been making her so tense. It was the prospect of meeting her mother.

While I had been growing up in the U.S., my mother had told me stories about my grandmother. All through my mother's childhood, Grandmother had been an uncaring and domineering figure for my mother. She never loved her daughters but favored her sons instead. She would not allow my mother to play with her friends and yelled at her incessantly, forcing my mother to do all the rigorous chores around the house while allowing her sons to rest and be pampered.

My mother's worst memory was of an event when she was a young girl. She used to accompany Grandmother on errands on dark nights through the entangled vegetation of their rural countryside. One night they were confronted by a pack of wild dogs, and my grandmother put my mother in front of her. Using my mother for her own protection, she had little concern for her daughter's safety.

Even now, as the matriarch of my mother's large family, she was used to ordering people around. She expected all her nine children to take care of her well and would capriciously complain about anything that displeased her.

When she opened the car door, my mother said to Grandmother, "*Sawadee*, Mother. How are you? I'm so very glad to see you are well. I'm so happy to see you!" Old habits took over. My mother's tense expression transformed into one of filial joy.

Grandmother's expression didn't change much. Except for a brief smile, she returned to a passive demeanor.

Plopped down on the vinyl seat within the shade of the car sat this great mass of a human being. Her scant and short wavy hair closely covered her round head. She had an indifferent expression upon her face as she patiently sat, gazing straight ahead and holding a cane in her wrinkled, plump right hand.

"This," my mother then turned to me and said, "is your yai." *Yai* is the Thai word for "maternal grandmother."

Immediately I slapped my hands together. "*Sawadee ca, Yai*." Grandmother merely smiled and said nothing.

I took my place next to her in the backseat of the car while my mother and sister went to sit in front with my uncle. Grandmother allowed my mother and her brother to talk on excitedly up front while she just listened from the back.

Being a meek and scrawny twelve-year-old, I felt overwhelmed to sit so close to the huge, corpulent person of my grandmother. Like an ancient queen from the past, her austere presence dominated and intimidated me.

When I noticed some dark reddish-orange stains on her tiny teeth, I began to feel afraid, too. The reddish-orange substance even streamed down the wrinkles at the corners of her mouth. My first thought was that her mouth had been bleeding and had not yet fully healed. But I saw that Grandmother kept a little basket on the floor by her feet. In it was a jar of a reddish-orange abrasive substance—I later learned from my mother it was a limestone derivative—packs of wide dried and fresh betel leaves, a knife, and a little clay spittoon.

Stooping down to her basket on the floor, she reached for a knife and slowly lifted it to the glass jar of limestone paste. The paste had a strange medicinal odor to it. She then picked up a wide, dry betel leaf from the packs of fresh and dry leaves. Placing the single leaf gently on her palm, she spread the paste on it with a knife, rolled it up into a tight little bundle, and put it in her mouth. After chewing it rapidly, she deposited it into the clay spittoon. I realized the betel juice created the reddish-orange stains on her mouth.

Unable to stand the uncomfortable silence any longer, I felt myself compelled to say something.

"What's it for?" I asked her, very curious about this strange ritual. "Is it some sort of medicine?"

I stared up at her curiously. Grandmother struck me as quite a strange character. Although she was only in her sixties, her face sagged and looked worn. Flat, round, wrinkled, and tan, it resembled the pinched-in face of a Pekinese dog.

Noticing my stare, Grandmother rolled her eyes downward but did not answer.

"Is it some sort of tobacco?" I persisted. "Why do you chew on it?"

"It's called mag. Mostly old people chew on it," she replied in a casual manner. She noticed neither my repulsion nor my curiosity. "Children mustn't ask so many questions," she added, as the reddish-orange abrasive liquid spattered her lips. She then resumed her silence.

Grandmother appeared to be a stern and cruel old woman, mean and selfish like any other bitter old woman. She was a brooding giant who just sat there listening to others enthusiastically conversing. I thought she might have been eavesdropping for information about her children throughout their conversation in order to use it later in pitting them against one another. Grandmother was infamous for stirring up conflict among her children.

Out of respect and fear, I kept my inquiries to a minimum and sat quietly unless spoken to. I figured if I didn't say much, others, and Grandmother in particular, would have little to say about me.

Finally our caravan arrived at Aunt Aiw's home. Protected by a steel gate and tall white walls, the house stood inside surrounded by neatly trimmed lawns. It was a spacious, modern, two-story house located in a residential area of the city. Our cars parked under the overhang in front of the house's door. As everyone got out of their cars and began to unpack, people moved hastily up and down the doorsteps, in and out of the house. Trunks and doors slammed amid the chatter of voices and thumping of luggage upon the ground.

Grandmother demanded that people assist her in getting out of the car. Her corpulence and bad right leg made it difficult for her to maneuver herself in and out of cramped places.

Immediately my uncle and aunt stopped, dropped the luggage they were carrying and rushed to help her.

"How do you expect me to get out of this car?" Grandmother scolded them. "My leg isn't as good as yours. Watch where you're going with me. I could fall down any moment, you know," she puffed.

I tried to disregard her complaints by focusing my attention on the whereabouts of my hippo. It was not in sight. Becoming worried, I went to the trunk of the car that was supposed to have contained it. To my relief it was still there, and I quickly snatched it up. Cradling it in my arms, I took it into the house.

As soon as we were all inside Aunt Aiw's house, my mother opened the suitcases that contained the gifts for our relatives. American dolls, clothing, chocolates, and electrical gadgets were soon strewn all over the living-room floor. Proudly I placed the hippo in the very center of the pool of presents. I could sense the delight of my relatives as they whispered to each other about the doll's cuteness.

I scanned the room for Cousin Owp. Although I had never seen her, I knew she was as old as me and looked for someone close to my age. I expected her to be over-joyed at receiving such a doll. A group of girls dressed in school uniforms of white blouses and black pleated skirts gathered at a corner of the room giggling and squirming with delight. Cousin Owp must be in that crowd, I thought, and couldn't wait to present her with my gift. In my excitement I had forgotten my grandmother. Without any expression on her stoic face, she scanned all the gifts. I ignored her and was just about to reach back for the hippo in order to hand it to the group of girls, when Grandmother suddenly spoke.

"Adorable," she said.

I turned to see her seated like an empress in a plush, comfortable armchair.

"It's adorable," she said through orange-stained lips. "May I have it to keep in my room? It's much too big for any child." She was already holding out her arms expec-tantly.

I looked in silent appeal to my mother, wanting her to stand up and tell Grandmother she couldn't have it. In-stead, my mother averted her eyes and smiled at Grand-mother respectfully.

Reluctantly, I picked up the hippo and made my way across the room, handing it to her with an insincere smile. Clutching it to herself, she rose with difficulty from her throne and took it immediately to her room.

She only confirmed the selfish and mean image of her I had previously formulated in my mind. What use did a sixty-year-old lady have for a stuffed animal? She was just greedy and domineering, I thought. A hippo to suit a hippo.

The gifts gradually dwindled as everyone took a little something. Moments later, Grandmother returned and claimed much of the candy we had brought. She filled her arms with as many boxes of chocolates as she could carry and headed once again back to her room. She didn't leave enough to give everyone else an equal share. What a bully for a woman so advanced in age, I thought. However, I did not criticize or complain aloud, out of respect for my elders. I also preferred to avoid conflict. When Grandmother was safely out of earshot, I turned to my mother.

"Why is she so stingy? I wanted to have enough gifts for everyone. She hoarded it all," I protested excitedly.

"You know how old people can get. They want to save everything," responded my mother.

"But she's lived such a long life—she should let other people have a chance to enjoy things too," I objected. "Besides, you can't take any of it with you when you're gone."

"That's true. Just don't take her so seriously. She's old; let her have her way," my mother said.

"How can you stand this?" I protested. "It's just not fair. After all she's put you through, how can you even stand her?" I insisted.

"She's still my mother, no matter what," my mother responded, plain and simple. "Without her, I would not have been born in this world. You must respect your elders and learn to forgive. If you cannot change her, you have no other choice but to accept her unconditionally."

Though I tried to accept my mother's advice, it did not prevent me from thinking of Grandmother as a wretched, evil old bully.

As the week passed, I saw Grandmother periodically when she'd drop by Aunt Aiw's house, where she was accommodated with a room all of her own. Then one day we actually went to visit her at her house remotely located in the outskirts of the city. I couldn't believe we were going to so much trouble after all she had done. I could just picture her sitting atop her heap of goods, never being satisfied, always wanting more. Why visit someone who needed no one? Such a greedy, bitter old woman deserved to be alone.

Isolated and hidden in the midst of the lush, green tropical vegetation of Thailand, my grandmother's house rose upon unstable wooden stilts. Although it was located within the vicinity of army barracks, when I stood upon the little porch, I could see only the pristine surroundings of abundant banana trees and emerald-green tall grasses. The house itself hardly seemed ordinary at all. It seemed insulated by the muted beauty that enveloped it without. The rooms, dark and dank with the smell of aged moist wood, were small and quaint but not confining. Glass windows were nonexistent, for there was no need for them in the all-engulfing humidity. Although lacking the modern amenity of air-conditioning, my grandmother's house was not uncomfortable. An occasional breeze would drift by to soothe our moist skins, relieving us from the humidity that drenched us in a thin film of perspiration.

The rooms were tidy and well kept. How such a sluggish woman was able to keep things neat and clean escaped me. Relics of Grandmother's past existed in every room. The ubiquitous scent of Grandmother's familiar limestone paste and betel leaves permeated the rooms. Atop an old, dusty teakwood dresser stood faded, yellowed, black-and-white photographs of my grandmother's children, her deceased husband, and herself. I could hardly believe that the thin, beautiful, delicate-featured young lady within the frame was the same woman who many years later was a grandmother withered and embittered by old age.

Curious to detect a remnant of that youth in my grandmother, I tried to get another glance at her.

Grandmother had planted herself outside upon her porch, chewing the usual leaves and paste. As the rest of my family drifted about inside the house, chatting and preparing for lunch, I ventured outside to sit with her.

She had brought the hippo home with her. At the sight of the hippo sitting morosely next to her on a cushioned sun chair, I lost all my hopes that she could be anything but a selfish old woman.

I sat staring out into the serene landscape, listening to the faint sound of crickets chirping from the nearby trees. Grandmother remained as speechless and still as the hippo next to her. In mutual silence we gazed out into the vast distance without acknowledging each other's presence even though we were only a few feet apart.

While she seemed to be in a trance, I stole a glance at

her. Although withered by age and the merciless scorching sun of Thailand, my grandmother's face appeared benign and almost childlike at that moment. I found it hard to believe that this old woman who appeared so harmless and subdued was the same woman who had caused so much toil and suffering in my mother's childhood. This was the same woman my mother had shed tears over when she recalled her mother's tyrannical dominance and lack of love. She was also the same woman who appeared so lovely and kind in the picture within. I began a trivial conversation with her.

"I've never seen a house like this before. It's very nice," I said. "How long have you been living here?"

"Too long. Your uncle bought it for me. But I'm old and will need to live near my children soon," she said, looking at me with aged, tired eyes. "Nowadays I hardly spend time here." The words flowed out of her mouth in a listless manner without emotion or concern.

"I wouldn't mind living here. I love it—it would be such fun," I responded, being more interested in my own adventures. My eyes lowered to examine the cracks and crevices on the wooden floor planks and then stared aimlessly beyond into the distance. I did not pay much attention to what she had to say.

"You have grown so much. It seems like just yesterday that you were but an infant. As a toddler, you were really playful and always wanted your own way," she said.

"Oh, really? I don't remember, but I hope I've changed," I replied, thinking it was ironic that Grandmother of all people should discuss such a personality trait with me.

"Time, it goes by so fast. People come into the world just as fast as they go out." Her voice faded into a gentle sigh that seemed to echo in the muted sounds of the tropical rain forest.

"Yes, I guess so," I said idly, still trying to maintain a distance from her—yet finding myself slowly being drawn to her. My perception of her was becoming muddled, and I didn't know what to think of her now.

"I won't be living in this world for very much longer," she said, ruminating over her imminent and fast-approaching death. "Everything must go someday."

I said nothing, not knowing how to respond to this unexpected revelation.

"And I'll have to go too," said Grandmother as her hand groped outward, taking the hippo by her side and hugging it to herself.

In her childlike gesture, I caught a glimpse of the young, slim girl in the faded photos of years long past.

As my conversation with my grandmother progressed, I noticed a faint teardrop trickle slowly down her plump, tanned cheek. The woman I had thought of as a stone actually did possess sentimental human feelings.

"Don't cry, Yai." I moved my chair closer to her, inching my way gradually toward her. "You mustn't be afraid. I think everything will be all right."

Looking at her aged old face, knowing that she could not escape what she so helplessly feared, I tried to comfort her with what I could.

"I don't know what will happen when we go," I said. "I'm afraid too."

"I will never see you, anyone, or anything ever again,"

she whimpered. "All these lovely trees, flowers, and clouds will be lost to me forever," she uttered in resignation.

"You're not alone now. . . . since we're both scared," I said. "I'm afraid too. We can be afraid together."

I began to guess the thoughts going through her mind—the guilt, fear, regrets of a long-endured life. Suddenly I held no grudge against her and no longer harbored any hatred for her. Instead, I found myself empathizing with her. I began to cry with her too.

Grandmother slowly released the hippo she had been holding so tightly and opened her plump arms toward me, and we embraced, holding on to each other as long as we could. I gasped at being held so tightly up against her warm, soft, gelatinous body.

We now shared a bond. Age had subdued Grandmother, but her greed was a desperate attempt to grasp life as long as possible. I could forgive my grandmother for her impertinent, childlike behavior and selfishness. It was a means of preserving the life that was so dear to her. With death, she would have to relinquish her domineering powers and no longer be the center of her children's pampering.

As human beings, I realized, we all share the same fate in death. All we have in life is each other and that means everything in the world. Grandmother was not an immutable stone of evil. She had insecurities she had to come to terms with, being just as weak as I or anyone else was, and fearing the oblivion that would come with death.

After that, my grandmother and I had a tacit understanding between us that allowed us to get along very well together. I became a favorite grandchild—despite her avowed preference for males. When anyone would pick on me, Grandmother would stand up in my defense. "She's my little girl," she'd say. "She always knows what she's doing. Go pick on someone else." I welcomed her commanding nature this time since it now revealed a glimmer of affection. All Grandmother really wanted and needed was compassion. I had listened to her when the others had ignored her, unraveling what others considered unfathomable in her.

When it came time to leave Thailand, everyone was saddened by our departure. Grandmother came to send us off too. The stern and indifferent woman I had first met at this airport had been replaced with a sobbing human being openly expressing her feelings.

"When will I see you again? I hope I live long enough for that day to come," said Grandmother in a mellow and sorrowful voice.

"You can come visit us in the States, Yai," I said.

"I don't know. It's difficult for me to get around, but I want to very much. We'll see what happens. Don't be afraid."

Her embrace was shaky as a result of the overwhelming emotions that caused her to tremble. It was as though a giant earthquake had opened up the depths of a mountain that had been solid for so long.

ANN TASHI SLATER is a Tibetan-American writer currently living in Tokyo.

THERE'S NO REASON TO GET ROMANTIC

So I'm sitting here in the cool eucalyptus shade of another sunny California afternoon, sipping iced tea and swinging my feet so the plum polish on my toenails will dry faster, and wondering how long this delicious period of grace will last. That is, I'll be far from surprised to hear the roar of the motor as my mother rounds the corner in her red Alfa Romeo, my grandmother gripping the passenger door with her bejeweled fingers.

"I probably shouldn't have bought that car," my mother said last night as I was undressing. She leaned against the doorjamb, the hallway light shining through her nightie, revealing her girlish shape.

"Who cares?" I said. "You didn't buy the car for her."

My mother looked at me sharply. "You know how much I detest that tone of voice."

I shrugged. And looked away before she could see my mouth pull down at the corners, the way it always does when she talks to me like that. As far as I can tell, it's not so much my tone of voice that makes my mother so testy—it's my grandmother's visiting from India. It's

185

especially bad right after my grandmother delivers her "You must be productive, you must not spend all your time shopping and sleeping, there's no use crying over spilt milk" speech. The spilt milk being my father. I've never been sure if my grandmother's attitude is the result of her Tibetan Buddhist belief in karma or of her never having been wild about my father in the first place, his being an American and a free-lance (i.e., unstable) journalist and all.

If it's a good day, my mother will point to me and say, "Alexis is evidence of my productivity." If it's a bad day, one of the days when my mother doesn't get dressed and cries in front of my father's picture, they argue and my grandmother says she doesn't know what she did to deserve such a lazy daughter.

"You used to be such a hard-working girl," my grandmother scolds. "Always doing all your lessons, helping your mummy. Now just look what has become of you." This only makes my mother cry more. Sometimes my grandmother cries then too. I usually go for a walk.

My toenails now are dry. I walk around on the cool cement of the breezeway, then open the screen door and lie faceup across the threshold with my head on the stairs. The sky is that deep, cool California blue, a wide azure sea, mine for the swimming. I follow a circling hawk, then close my eyes and launch myself upwards into that feathered black body, and I'm almost convinced that I'm looking way, way down at my bony, dark legs and curly black hair when the roar rises like the first wave of a storm. I jump to my feet and pull the screen door closed, sweep my nail polish and cotton balls into the skirt of my dress, and run for my room with delicate leaps like a deer in the woods. Before I even reach the top of the stairs, I hear their voices.

"You mustn't drive so fast," says my grandmother, her voice soft, singsong. "It's very dangerous, you know. In Sitla just this year we have had many fatalities, what with these ruffians speeding here and there with no concern for others. And what's more, these ones who get into accidents are always absconding."

"They *abscond* because otherwise the bystanders will stone them to death," my mother snaps. "And anyway, I was *not* speeding. We can't crawl along at a snail's pace. Don't you understand it's just as dangerous to go under the speed limit?"

I'm dying to get down to my room, but I wait, wanting to hear more. At the thought of My Mother, the Ruffian, I get a fit of the giggles, and the only way I can keep quiet is to think of something very serious and sad. I imagine my grandmother dying, and right away the laughter's gone. But then just as quickly I see my grandmother in her silk Tibetan dress, the gauzy sleeves of the underblouse pressed against her soft flesh as my mother takes the corner in her Alfa like there's no tomorrow, and again I'm dissolving in laughter.

When my grandmother was born five hundred years ago in a little town in Tibet, I'm sure no one even dreamed she'd end up charging around Marin County, California (a.k.a. Hip/Cool County), in the passenger seat of a red Alfa driven by her *daughter* no less! My mother hates when I exaggerate, but I say five hundred years because it truly seems like my grandmother's been around forever, like her silky, wrinkled face has seen everything that ever happened or might happen. I mean, when she was a girl, she rode on a yak over the Himalayas to reach India—giving up Tibetan butter tea for English breakfast tea because that was when India was still a British colony. The only things we ever ride on here are bicycles and windsurfers.

I told Cory about the yak and now she's dying to meet my grandmother, because Cory's the type with romantic ideas about faraway places. I told her my grandmother's very busy though, and there probably won't be time for them to meet.

Maria Hsu wants to come over also, and my mother even suggested that I invite her, probably because she feels guilty. After Tiananmen Square, my mother seemed to have a kind of epiphany, you know, like she doesn't lump all the Chinese into one big group anymore.

Being a devout Buddhist, my grandmother's always had a compassionate attitude towards the Chinese even with all that they've done to the Tibetans. But my mother—maybe it's been too long since she sat on prayer cushions with her brothers and sisters in the family altar room. Or maybe she started hating them after hearing the stories of torture and murder straight from my father's mouth when he returned from reporting assignments over there.

Anyway, another reason it seems like my grandmother's been around forever is because she's been around forever in *my* life. From day one she's been in my face, making me sit next to her for hours and knead dough for Tibetan steamed dumplings; trying to teach me the Tibetan script (finally she gave up, telling me I write "like a chicken"—it was only the other day that I realized she'd probably heard the phrase "chicken scratch" and was making it her own); forcing me to recite the Tibetan mantra "Om Mani Padme Hum," which means basically "Hail to the Buddha" and which I kept pretending to forget until she told my mother one day she was worried I might be "mental"; writing me frequent advisory or nostalgic letters between her yearly visits to America: "Don't give boys the cow, otherwise they will know they can enjoy the milk"—like a secret code that only I know means "Don't let a boy past second base."

When I was little it was the pinch-on-the-cheek routine and "You're a cheeky brat," and now it's "You're fifteen years and you must start being of some use to your darling mother." Sometimes I wonder where my grandmother gets off talking to me like that, and then I think it must be because my grandfather died soon after they were married, leaving her to raise eight children. That kind of thing makes you tough.

You know how they say "Like father, like son?" Well, like mother, like daughter. My father died just before I was born—am I doomed to marry someone who's going to, as my grandmother says, leave one fine day before the harvest bounty can be reaped? (She has poetic inclinations.) Maybe not, though, because I'm the first half-breed in the family, my mother being the only one who married a non-Tibetan. She hates when I say "half-breed," but there's no reason to get romantic. The truth is that I'm half and half, and no matter what they teach us in math class, I often wonder if two halves really do make a whole.

I step carefully on one end of the top stair, hoping it won't creak. The wood makes no noise at all, but my grandmother's voice shoots out from the kitchen: "Alexis, is that you?"

I stop and hold my breath, but hearing her slow step across the linoleum, I answer, "Yes, who else would it be?" The "yes" is a concession because she's always trying to get me to say "yes" instead of "yeah," but the rest is pure cheeky brat.

"We've just come back from the store," my grandmother says, as if this is news to me, appearing around the corner and looking at me like she always does—that is, not really looking but *inspecting*. "What is that you've done to your toes?" she asks, peering at my feet like they're little animals.

I know better than to try to answer. Though I contemplate staring at her beautifully polished fingernails and saying "What is that you've done to your fingers?"

"Why don't you wear a brassiere with that dress?" she says severely, her face puckering into a frown. "That is very vulgar. You must keep yourself covered."

I glance at the small bumps on my chest that pass for breasts. I say nothing.

She smiles and shakes her head, then takes hold of my hair and lifts it high. "What is it you've done to your nice, straight hair?" she asks, as if she's asking for the first time, as if I got my hair permed today, not two months ago, as if she hasn't been seeing me every day for three weeks. "You American girls like these funny-looking styles, isn't it?"

I step back and bend over like I'm bowing to her, trying to pull my hair from her hands without leaving any in her grasping fingers. In spite of the promise I made to my mother not to fight with my grandmother this time, I can't help saying, "How come whether I'm American, Tibetan or somewhere in between depends on what you feel like saying?" I deliver this in my low, snake voice, so my mother won't hear. I know I always regret being mean to my grandmother, but whether or not her life's been hard, and even if I am younger than she is, I deserve at least a little respect.

"You are still such a difficult girl," my grandmother says now, letting go of my hair and shaking her finger at me. We're still standing in the hallway, me with one foot on the stair again. "You American girls have a mind of your own, isn't it?" she continues.

"I do *not* have a mi—" I stop short, furious. Always she comes up with these tricky things, forcing me to say things that leave me looking stupid. I make a tight little ball out of the cotton and nail polish still in the skirt of my dress. "Why are you always trying to describe me?" I say then, twisting the dress so hard I'm surprised it doesn't rip. Besides, I think, you have to take credit for some of me, for some of this contrariness.

It's you who's told me stories of Bonpo sorcerers, of ancient shamans crippling people with choking spells—it's no coincidence that unlike normal girls, I've gone about with wicked thoughts, not crying before people like Robby Molnar who call me Ching Chong Chinaman in the schoolyard but wanting instead to destroy them.

Later in the afternoon, while my grandmother's taking her nap, my mother comes and sits at the top of the stairs with her coffee, the way she does when she wants to talk. "Allie," she begins, calling me by my pet name, and I know she's going to say something I don't want to hear.

I examine my toenail polish and wonder if I should put on another coat.

"Allie, I know it's not always easy for you when your grandmother's here visiting . . ."

"That's the understatement of the year." I wait for her to explode, but she doesn't bite. And you're not one to talk, I want to say; but for a change, I keep my mouth shut. My mind starts to wander, the way it does sometimes when I'm nervous, and I imagine my mother's a goddess like the one in the Tibetan painting on silk she keeps in the hallway, wearing a necklace made of human bone, and it almost looks like her own bones are showing through her skin. I hear the clink of her coffee cup on the saucer (or maybe it's the sound of bone on bone?): The goddess is sipping coffee.

Then she sighs, and she's no longer supernatural, just the slender woman who one boiling afternoon in Calcutta spilled her drink on my father at the Great Eastern Hotel (and the rest, as they say, is history), whose luminous face no doubt came to him as he bobbed in the green waves of the San Francisco Bay and then drifted slowly to the bottom. Sometimes my mother creeps downstairs at night, crying, and as she falls back asleep against my side, I lie awake and know that part of her rests on the sea floor, her long black hair flowing like seaweed, and another part is back in Calcutta, and still another in Sitla amidst the snow-covered Himalayas, steaming Tibetan dumplings, New Year's picnics under traditional blue-and-white tents, family pilgrimages by train to Bodh Gaya, ballroom dancing with soldiers on leave. And the other parts of her, who knows where they might be.

"What I'm trying to say, Allie, is that your grandmother's only here for a short time, and she's getting older. . . . Maybe you could try a little harder to be nice to her? You always forget how terrible you feel after she's gone for not being nicer to her. So why not make a little more effort? It's not that hard, is it?"

I'm checking my toenail polish again but this time I can't see very well because of course my mother's right and the tears are stinging my eyes.

My mother goes out to buy a jazz CD she saw reviewed in the newspaper. I tiptoe down the hall, cringing under the gaze of the fierce goddess on silk, and peek in the door of my grandmother's room. She's sleeping propped up against two fluffy pillows, her prayer beads resting loosely in her hands, a photograph of my grandfather on the bedside table next to a silver prayer wheel. Her wispy black hair lies across the pillow like a miniature horse's tail; her skin droops over the slack muscles of her jaw.

She shifts in her sleep and, without opening her eyes, begins counting her beads again. I step back, ready to run, but my presence goes undetected.

Suddenly my grandmother appears unfamiliar, in the same way a word becomes strange, unknowable, the more times you repeat it. I stare at her and see, like a black-and-white movie reel unwinding, that long-ago procession through town on horseback, my grandmother in Tibetan bridal dress, her hair entwined in an intricate headpiece of turquoise, coral and pearls. And then back even further, I see her as a girl of thirteen astride a yak, leaving Tibet with her family for the unknown world beyond, on the lookout for bandits, awakened in the night by the battling ghosts of Tibetan and Chinese soldiers.

My grandmother crossed the mountains, my mother the ocean—I want to know where my journey is. If I leave behind climbing the Golden Gate Bridge at night and camping on the beach and weekly trips to Berkeley to see *The Rocky Horror Picture Show*, where will I go? But then why *should* I go, why is it that my mother and grandmother are always wanting me to be something I am not? I stand by the door for a few more minutes, watching my grandmother slowly, gently count her beads of bone, and wonder if it's really possible that I'm related by blood to this tiny woman murmuring in a language I do not know.

Downstairs in my room, I peer into the mirror, looking for my grandmother. But aside from the semi-flat nose, the dark, dark eyes I've so often wished were blue, the black hair I've wanted to dye blond, she eludes me. Quickly, before I can change my mind, I run to the bathroom and pull out the dye I've kept for so long.

———

"What on earth were you thinking?" my mother hisses after dinner, pushing me towards the sink to do the dishes. "It looks awful, and at least you could have waited until your grandmother left."

"God, Mom, you act like I shaved my head," I say, filling the dish tub with hot water. "I only dyed the roots, and besides, it seems to bother you a lot more than her." To my complete surprise, my grandmother had smiled as I sat down at the table, and simply said, "Oh, just see what she's done to her hair," before launching into a story about the strange dream she had during her afternoon nap.

"Shut up. You shut up." My mother's putting the left-overs into the fridge.

"Why don't you say it louder so she can hear you?" I ask in my trumpet voice. My grandmother's in the other room watching the evening news. "There's nothing to hide," I continue. "We're all one big family, right?"

In a flash, my mother crosses the linoleum and smacks me across the face.

At the next moment, my grandmother enters the kitchen, smiling innocently, and says, "Shall we have some dessert? My doctor says that I must eat at least one serving of fruit each day."

I want to throw the hot water at both of them, but I don't move, hoping my grandmother will notice the welt on my cheek.

"Let's have some of those wikis, shall we?" my grand-mother says, crossing to the fruit bowl. "We don't get these in Sitla, you know."

"KIWIS!" I shout. "They're KIWIS! Don't you know anything? Don't either of you know anything?!" They stare at me like I'm from outer space, my grandmother holding a kiwi in each hand, my mother clenching and unclenching her fists.

I whip the dishcloth across the room and rush downstairs. Without taking off my clothes, I crawl into bed and for a long time I stare at the ceiling, remembering how I used to fantasize about killing myself. The problem was that I wouldn't be around for the satisfaction of watching my mother and grandmother grieve, and this obstacle was enough to keep me from actually trying anything. Maybe there was the possibility of being reincarnated, as my grandmother believes, but I'd have lost so much merit by killing myself that I'd probably have come back as an ant or a tree stump.

At last I drift off to sleep. I dream that I'm a scribe in the middle of a huge complex of stone buildings and walkways, an ancient monastic city trembling with the voices and cries of thousands of red-robed Tibetan monks. Far, far above, at the top of a great pyramid, surveying the realm, sits a golden female Buddha on a blue lotus throne. I hunch over my Tibetan script, hoping not to be noticed, but I'm given an assignment: It's now my job to dive deep down into the murky waters of the realm and bring things to the surface. Because I have no choice, I dive. I wriggle past the worn busts of my mother and father, slowing for a moment but then quickly reversing towards the light. Surfacing, I learn that I've been sentenced to death, that my heart will be cut out on the sacrificial stone at the top of the pyramid. But there is no human sacrifice in Tibet, I think, and there aren't even any pyramids. However, again I am summoned, and because I have no choice, I begin the long climb up the narrow, steep stairs to my death. When at last I reach the top, I see a dark-haired woman lounging on a dais, smiling and humming to herself. Well, there's no reason not to try, I think.

"Excuse me," I begin in a quiet, soft voice. "Is there any possibility of a reprieve?"

"Sure," says the woman casually, matter-of-factly. "Wait there in the back." She points behind her with her thumb to a vast grassy area punctuated by white columns so tall they seem to be holding up the cloudless blue sky. I stretch out on the ground, noticing the warm breeze, people lolling on the grass, perhaps picnicking, and I'm amazed that a place like this exists.

I wake up much earlier than usual, so early that it isn't yet light and the birds are just beginning to chirp. Though my mother will be asleep for hours yet, I bound up the stairs—now a great, lithe cat with sure step—and down the hall towards the room where already my grandmother's awake. I know of course that she's been up for an hour, maybe more, counting her beads, reading, paging through her photo albums, writing letters. It is one of the paradoxes of life, she always says, that when you are young and want to do many things, you need more sleep than when you are old and the hours pass slowly. Time grows very heavy, she says, like a drop of water about to burst.

I don't want to bother her, so I keep it brief and talk fast. Maybe a little too fast, but I'm nervous: "I forgot to tell you that my friend Cory . . . and Maria"—it's only at this moment that I really do want Maria to come over and suddenly my chest feels very big, like there's all this space inside—"they, um, want to meet you and I was wondering if they could come over today, if you have any free time, that is." I push my toenails into the pale-blue carpet.

My grandmother slowly closes her book, peers at the clock on her bedside table, and then at me.

The lithe, cat feeling is gone, and I feel scrunched and hunched like some kind of dwarf, but I stand my ground.

"Yes, yes, let them come," my grandmother says then with a sweet smile.

For some reason, god knows why, I shrug my shoulders and stare stupidly. Crossing my signals, I guess. I've practiced shrugging and looking exasperated so many times, but in the clutch I come up with this aborted version. My grandmother probably thinks I'm stranger than ever now, but she says nothing, only returns to her book. In some way that I appreciate, this is just like her, just like the way she accepts the occasional nocturnal visits of long-dead friends and relatives.

So Cory and Maria come over, so excited you'd think the Queen of England was at my house, and, of all things, my grandmother wants us to help her dye her hair because the grey is starting to show again.

I've never before helped my grandmother with her hair, but today, from the moment my mother straggled down to the kitchen in her filmy nightie and fumbled with the coffee maker, I could see that she was going to spend the day on the edge. It's hard to blame her, considering the mother and daughter she has. So I told her, go ahead and do what you need to do today, the three of us will keep Grandmother company. She's roared off to the beach in the Alfa, tires screeching.

Now it's relatively peaceful here in the bathroom, my grandmother surrounded by me and Cory and Maria, facing the mirror. Cory's chattering away like a little bird, asking my grandmother all sorts of questions, and it doesn't even upset me that she's finding out things I've never bothered to ask about.

Maria's alternately holding my grandmother's hand and, in that shy, sweet way she has, examining my grandmother's turquoise and coral rings, her wine-colored nails. Occasionally my grandmother pats Maria's hand while saying something to Cory, and it doesn't bother me that my grandmother and I do not touch each other like that.

I take care to spread the dye evenly, paying special attention to the roots. Cory, Maria, and my grandmother are in their element. I press my fingers to the back of my grandmother's head as I put a bit more dye on the top, and I'm startled at how delicate her bones are, how familiar the contours of her skull. Eyes closed, I spread my fingers more firmly against her hair and it seems that I'm touching my own head again, touching my own roots. The similarity is so strong and surprising that I quickly open my eyes, certain that Cory and my grandmother will have noticed something odd, but they're talking away, and Maria's still examining. Again I close my eyes, and this time I gently move my hands, tracing a terrain that is, after all, known to me.

AMY LING *is a Chinese American poet and educator.*

GRANDMA LING

If you dig that hole deep enough,
you'll reach China, they used to tell me,
a child in a backyard in Pennsylvania.
Not strong enough to dig that hole,
I waited twenty years,
then sailed back, half way around the world.

In Taiwan I first met Grandma.
Before she came to view, I heard
her slippered feet softly measure
the tatami floor with even step;
the aqua paper-covered door slid open
and there I faced
my five foot height, sturdy legs and feet,
square forehead, high cheeks and wide-set eyes;
my image stood before me,
acted on by fifty years.

She smiled, stretched her arms
to take to heart the eldest daughter
of her youngest son a quarter century away.
She spoke a tongue I knew no word of,
and I was sad I could not understand,
but I could hug her.

GRANDMA TRAUB

Everything about her said, "Surplus":
extra chins, flaps of loose flesh,
flocks of freckles,
here and there a wart;
her dresses yards of georgette
set off with brooches,
twisted strands of pearls;
her white hair, sometimes dyed blue
to keep the yellow out, rolled up
round her head like a halo.

Love too she had in surplus,
left her own Pennsylvania Dutch
to sail clear to China
brought the Bible and modern medicine,
became head nurse,
director of Yoyang hospital,
adopted my mother when her mother died.

Retired and back home,
in sensible low heels
black and laced up high,
behind round wire-rimmed glasses
her blue eyes delighted in us,
her Chinese grandchildren.
She tucked us into her home,
cooked shoo fly pie, fresh donuts,

dandelion salads, tapioca puddings;
read Bambi, Heidi, Pollyanna,
transformed leftover cloth
into flowers for our quilts.

For Christmas and birthdays,
she was giving me one at a time
a wedding party of dolls:
the tall bride in proud white satin,
bridesmaids in rose and powder blue.
She was just making a suit
for the undersized groom,
this large woman who never married,
when she died.

REBECCA HONMA *is a Japanese American writer who is also a reporter in Honolulu.*

JIJAN

*J*ijan, *tell me your dreams.*

The question floats to the surface of my mind as I stare at my grandfather's wooden pillow cradled in my lap.

I really don't expect an answer. I was thirteen when Grandfather died. He's been dead for twenty-five years. But every now and then something triggers another silent conversation.

This one starts because Grandfather's memorial service was held last Sunday afternoon. We assembled at the small wooden temple, still standing on its rickety foundations but so ravaged by termites that in several places the walls appeared paper thin.

We lit incense sticks, listened to the drone of the priest as he chanted the prayers, and wondered where all the years had gone. Decades before, the child in the pew creating simple hats and boats by folding sheets of paper had been myself. Last Sunday it was cousin Brenda's six-year-old.

After the service, we ended up at Sumi's Café for dinner. We talked about jobs, Uncle Kazu's latest trip to Las Vegas, and yet-to-be-born babies. No one really said much about Grandfather.

———

When I glanced at the tables, Jijan, I realized that more than half of the people there—counting the kids—never knew you. I guess it can't be helped. These days we don't live in the same place and sometimes we see each other just once a year. To many of them you're just an old photograph sitting on top of the television set.

My grandfather was not a fighter. I suppose he had enough nerve and curiosity within him to make the journey to Hawaii with others from his village.

But stories of exploits and stunning achievements in this new land were not part of his story.

Instead I remember Grandfather working in his garden, picking grasshoppers off rows of lettuce and the eggplant bush.

Or he would sit with me at the kitchen table in the dead stillness of the early afternoon, when I should have been napping, carrying out a silly game of pretend.

I would draw small lines and dashes in vertical columns on paper and he would then translate my "Japanese" into full-blown stories of magic cherry blossom trees and talking fish, always saying "*jozu, jozu,*" smart girl, smart girl.

Aside from that he never said much. But he loved words, filling dozens of our leftover school notebooks with his writing.

"You know, Jijan was the only one who wrote to me when I moved away," Auntie Fumie said a few years ago. "And he wrote in English because he knew my Japanese was useless."

It's too bad, Jijan, no one kept your letters or your books. I have nothing to unlock your silence or to coax you into speaking. With each passing year you seem to retreat further and further into the background. Until all I have left of you are fuzzy memories, childhood impressions.

In my mind, it is always late afternoon with the first shadows of the evening creeping into the dining room.

Grandfather is sitting next to the open window trying to take advantage of a slight breeze. You know it's going to be a warm night. Fat brown termites are beginning to swarm in the air.

Grandfather eats dinner alone, long after everyone has had their turn. The family is too large to sit at the table together, so we eat in shifts. But as always Grandfather eats last.

He holds a bowl of rice with one hand and with the other he deftly uses his chopsticks to pick up cold lumps of fried fish.

Even when darkness envelopes the room, none of the house lights are turned on. Grandmother says it's too hot for lights and the family really can't afford the bill.

"*Denki ga po ho*—the lights are a waste," she yells at me as I start to play with the switch.

And so the argument begins. I pick a fight with my grandmother and end up calling her names. We go on for several minutes until I notice that Grandfather has left the room.

He has gone to his bedroom to lie down and to listen to the scratchy *ra-tat-tat-tat* sounding broadcast of the local Japanese-language radio station.

Grandfather always used a pillow fashioned from a log, split in half and sanded down until splinters could no longer hurt the back of the neck.

Its smooth curved shape and honey brown color remind me of a loaf of bread.

I remember in Sunday School learning about Jacob and how he used a rock for his pillow. As he slept in an open field, Jacob dreamed of angels going up and down a ladder hung from heaven. Jijan, were your dreams as terrifying as Jacob's?

Even as Grandfather lay dying from pneumonia, he refused to trade his worn, ancient pillow for something softer.

He also kept quiet about the pain in his chest and the blood in his urine.

The doctor thought it was a translation problem.

"'The old man doesn't speak English too well and I don't speak Japanese,' that's what the doc told me," my father recalled later, shaking his head. "Maybe we could have done more."

Grandfather passed away so early in the morning that the stars were still visible in the sky. My mother took the telephone call and went to rouse my father, saying it was time.

I asked if I could come along, but my parents told me stay at home and wait. So I returned to bed and lay under the quilt, not knowing what to expect. The only sound I remembered hearing before drifting off to sleep was the howling of the village dogs as they began their nightly prowl.

No one was really surprised by the timing of Grandfather's death. But unlike those of a few others who had died in the village, grandfather's passing away had occurred without any forewarning or premonitions.

Jijan, do you remember Uncle Fred? A week before Uncle died, Bulatao man dreamed that he saw an old woman walking with a young boy dressed in his best clothes—a white shirt and black shorts. Mr. Bulatao told Auntie Emma about the dream, and when she showed him a snapshot of Grandma, he said that was the woman with the young boy. 'Ah missus, I think your mama came to take Fred,' he said.

Because I've heard enough of these stories, I half expect them to happen to me. And why shouldn't they, I ask; who else seems to be waiting for the past to speak, as if it were only a phone call away?

But it's different for Grandfather—I want something more. I want a good-bye.

As the family prepared the special food for Grandfather's funeral dinner, Auntie Mitsi told the rest of us what happened.

It took place half an hour after Grandfather had died, she said, although at the time Mitsi did not know of Grandfather's death.

"I heard knocking at the front door, so I got up to answer. Funny, nobody was there. Maybe the wind, I thought. So I go back to bed. But it happened again, the same thing. This time I left the porch light on."

We continued shaping the cooked rice into fist-sized balls; no one said a word.

My mother was the first to break the silence. "It was probably Jijan coming to tell you good-bye. No feel bad about not catching him—you know how he was. He hated to bother anyone."

Everyone else agreed, nodding their heads and sighing. A few of the women wiped their eyes with their aprons.

I wondered if I had missed Grandfather's visit and the chance to hear words he rationed out so carefully in his life.

As soon as the family was through observing the forty-nine days of mourning, I found Grandmother emptying all Grandfather's personal belongings into a healthy fire.

An old rusty barrel in the backyard served as the incinerator. It was often used to burn dry leaves and household trash.

From a distance, Grandmother looked as if she was performing an exotic purification ritual. But she was far more practical than she was religious.

She smiled as I approached the barrel. The sunlight glinted off the gold filling in her front tooth.

"Look, I make more room," she said, vigorously shaking the box full of writing tablets—Grandfather's diaries—into the flames. Next went his photographs and letters from Japan.

Grandfather's life was quickly turning into curly black ashes that floated above the smoking barrel.

I backed away from the fire and quietly entered the

house and made my way to the darkened bedroom. It smelled of dust and mothballs. The sweet odor of rotting fruit also drifted into the bedroom from an open window. Outside, several ripe mangoes lay oozing in the moist ground, their red-and-orange skins split apart by the fall from the tree.

I found Grandfather's pillow where it always was, lying at the head of his sagging bed. The mattress looked naked without the yellowing sheets and blankets.

A dark spot, the residue of more than sixty-five years of sweat and hair oil, stained the middle of the pillow.

I smuggled the pillow out of the bedroom by stuffing it into a large paper bag filled with rags. But my grandmother, who rarely missed a thing and despite her preoccupation with the fire, spotted me from across the yard. She wanted to know what was in my bundle.

I told her I had taken some rags to use for a mop.

"You show me what you take," she shouted back. "No worry," I answered. "I going bring 'em back." I turned and ran out of the yard. Minutes later, Grandmother telephoned my parents to complain about my lack of respect.

My grandmother realized the pillow was missing several months later. But her irritation escalated into fury when she discovered who had taken it. She accused her son—my father—and the rest of us of conspiring against her.

As for me, I'm called stupid for tampering with bad luck. "*Baka! baka! bachi*," she fumed.

My father finally cut her off and said we didn't believe in superstitious ramblings. Grandmother's eyes bulged as she gritted her teeth, turned around, and slammed the door behind her.

My parents could barely contain their laughter when they described the scene to other family members later. Even I began mimicking Grandmother's high-pitched voice and facial contortions.

But Jijan, tell me, is it true? Was I stupid for taking your pillow? Is that why you don't talk to me?

So I say I inherited the pillow, although some could justifiably accuse me of stealing it. You can interpret it any way you like, the outcome is the same. The pillow is mine. But with only a wooden pillow, how else can I make the connections for those still yet to come?

"Jozu jozu"—Jijan, that's all I have. Won't you tell me more?

WILLIAM F. WU *is a Chinese American writer who lives in southern California. He has a Ph.D. in American Culture and has had a story adapted for* The Twilight Zone. *His* Hong on the Range *was selected by the American Library Association as among the Best Books for Young People in 1989.*

BLACK POWDER

April, A.D. 2017: Star Hector Space Station.

Tom Leong, a seventeen-year-old high school junior, slumped back in his chair, staring at the English paper he had just received. On the side wall of the classroom, a large video screen continuously showed a view of Earth, which slowly changed as Star Hector orbited the planet. Even though Tom's family had lived here all of his life, he usually found the view distracting, but not today. Right now, everything only reminded him of his father.

The elder Tom Leong had been killed in a shuttle accident flying from here to the Moon on business just a few days ago. The cause of the accident had been a computer error from Moonbase. The funeral had taken place yesterday at their family's Episcopalian church on Star Hector.

Worst of all, the funeral had seemed completely impersonal. All the grown-ups had gone through some motions, and then afterward they had just stood around talking somberly about what a fine man Tom's father had been. It didn't seem to fit his dad. Tom's dad had been friendly, talkative, always smiling and joking.

Tom was pretty sure that every funeral in their church was exactly the same, with nothing personal about the deceased at all. He felt that his father deserved more. The funeral was over now, though.

Figures, he thought. *It just figures. Best grade I ever got in this lousy class. And I can't even show it to my dad.*

As Mr. Lebeau droned on about how this quarter's grades would be calculated, Tom stared at the B+ on his paper. It was unusually good for him, especially since he had written the entire paper the last day before it was due and most of that night. His father had been after him for the previous two weeks to get to work on it, warning him that the result would be garbage if he didn't put some effort into it.

At the time, angry, Tom had wanted to prove him wrong. That was over with. Now he just wished he could show it off to him.

Tom glanced up and saw Mr. Lebeau looking at him. He waited for a rebuke from the slender, curly-haired teacher for not paying attention. Instead, Mr. Lebeau just looked away and went on talking.

Tom felt worse. Last night he had cried for a while over losing his father, but he didn't want anyone feeling sorry for him. Determined to pretend that he was completely back to normal, he sat up in his seat and started listening.

Alvin Kwok pushed out of his chair, eased his weight onto his seventy-two-year-old legs carefully, and then grinned at his daughter, Ellen.

"I sure appreciate your moving away from the full-gravity section of Star Hector here to the half-gravity section just for me," he said. "Living here in one half the gravity of Earth just might do the trick for me, at least for a while."

Ellen, young Tom's mother, turned in the kitchen area with a weird-looking transparent pot in her hand. Her short black hair swayed around her face with the movement, floating in the half gravity. "Well, your doctor said it would relieve the amount of work your heart has to do. Besides, living in the one-gravity section was more expensive. I'm just glad Tom left enough insurance to . . . help." She shrugged with an awkward smile.

Alvin regretted reminding her of her husband's death, but then realized that it was constantly on her mind anyway. He nodded at the large, transparent object she was holding. "What, may I ask, is that thing?"

"Hm? Oh!" She laughed, a little too loudly. "This is a zero-gravity wok. You stir-fry in it."

"Why don't you use a regular wok?" He knew, but he wanted to keep her distracted from her grief for a moment longer. Playing the role of an ignorant old man wasn't too hard up here in space, where he had never traveled before this week. As soon as the accident had occurred, Ellen had arranged for him to come up for the funeral and then stay here to live.

"Well, you can't cook in an open container in zero

gravity; everything flies away. So somebody up here invented this. The basic shape is that of two woks, one on top of the other. See, they're hinged, so you can open it to put in oil and food and then close it for cooking. In zero gravity, you don't have to stir it; once the wok is heated, everything flies around inside real fast and all the food stirs itself."

"What's with the funny-looking handle?"

"You use this long, hollow handle to add stuff after it's hot. And you can smell from it to see how the dish is cooking. You microwave the whole thing, then you can look through the transparent surface to see how it's going."

"A brilliant invention," said Alvin, grinning. "But why do you have to use it here in half gravity?"

"Because there isn't really enough gravity to hold the food down at cooking temperature in a regular wok," said Ellen. "Not if you stir it." She had started taking out some chicken meat, grown from clones maintained on Star Hector, and some vegetables she had grown in a tank here in the cramped apartment. "When the food is heated up, it'll splatter and fly around in all directions."

"It does that on Earth, too," said Alvin. "Maybe somebody ought to start selling these down in Chinatown. Make a fortune."

A sound caught his attention, and he turned to see young Tom and his ten-year-old sister Lisa come in, walking with a casual bounce in the half gravity.

"Hi, kids," said Alvin.

"Hi, Grandpa," said Lisa, jumping toward him.

Alvin winced out of habit, anticipating her weight, then grinned in surprise to find that she was as light as a four-year-old as she landed on his lap. She clung to him hard. He decided not to mention the fact that he didn't like the word "Grandpa" much; that must be what they called their other grandfather. Years ago, he had addressed his own father's father as "Grandfather." He had always looked forward to being called that someday in his turn.

"Hi, Tom," Alvin said, looking over Lisa's shoulder.

"Hi," Tom muttered, moving on to his room without stopping.

Alvin let Lisa sit on his lap and tell him about her schoolday. Dinner was ready soon, and the four of them ate together. The conversation struck Alvin as stilted, but under the circumstances that was understandable.

"Tom," Alvin said, poking through his stir-fried chicken to find a mushroom. "Can you explain to me how this crazy space station works? How you can have some places with no gravity and some with half normal gravity and some with regular gravity?"

"Yeah, I guess." Tom shrugged. "It's shaped like a bicycle wheel and axle. The axle is called a spindle, and there's a hub around the middle. Then tubes that look like spokes go out to the wheels."

"More than one?"

"Yeah," said Lisa, looking back and forth between them. "Lots."

"The wheels are concentric," said Tom with bored patience. "The rest of the system is zero gravity, but the

215

wheels spin at different speeds. The faster they go, the more centrifugal force creates artificial gravity against the far inside wall, which is the floor here."

"Got it," said Alvin, nodding approval. "Thanks."

Tom reached for his third bowl of rice.

Alvin turned to Ellen. None of the others seemed to feel like talking, but he felt that a semblance of routine would be good for them. "What is it you do, exactly, up here?"

"Oh, Dad." Ellen laughed. "I told you last year, when I got the promotion. I'm a middle-level manager for Hector Vacuum Manufacturing. We make industrial equipment in zero gravity, like ball bearings. In space, you can get a perfect sphere." She sighed. "I have to make a trip in a few weeks to the Moon, myself. I'm not looking forward to it."

"Oh, wonderful," said Tom loudly. "The same flight Dad took?" He suddenly got up and actually leaped all the way into the living room, where he grabbed the corner of the wall and swung out of sight.

"Sorry," Ellen said apologetically.

Alvin shrugged.

"The same flight Dad took?" Lisa repeated, staring at her mother.

"No," Ellen said quickly. "I'll, um, make sure."

After dinner, Alvin sat in the living room in front of a news show, but was not paying much attention to it. This was a comfortable-enough home, though it was a far cry from Chicago's Chinatown, where he had been born and raised, and Flagstaff, Arizona, where he had spent most of his adult life. Of course, this would be his last home; he knew he was dying. His heart was weaker than ever, which was why his doctor had recommended a low-gravity environment a few months ago. Until his son-in-law's death, however, moving up here had not been feasible.

He felt guilty about that and hoped to repay the family a little by helping them through the transition—not to take the elder Tom's place, of course; that was impossible. Still, he had vague notions of making a contribution.

Alvin realized, suddenly, that young Tom was standing in the shadowed entrance from the hall, looking at the news on the video screen. His mother had gone out. Tom was nervously twisting some papers in his hands.

"Am I in your place?" Alvin asked, to draw him into conversation.

"No."

"Come sit down with me."

Reluctantly, Tom came and flopped back into a reclining chair. He ruffled the edges of the papers with one thumb. "My dad thought this was going to be real garbage."

"What is it? May I?" Alvin held out his hand.

"I got it back today." Tom gave it to him.

"'The Setting in *Bleak House* by Charles Dickens,'" Alvin read. "I may have read that book once. I don't remember. But Dickens is never a simple read, is he? Say, a B plus. Congratulations."

"Thanks," Tom said dully.

"You a good student, Tom?"

"Not really. I hate writing English papers. That's the best I ever did on one."

"That your worst subject?"

"Naw." He laughed nervously. "Chemistry. It's boring."

Alvin looked at the paper in his hand. "I'm sure your father would have been very proud."

"Yeah." Tom snickered. "That's what Mom said. I just wish I could have shown it to him."

"Well," Alvin said lamely, "perhaps he can see it from wherever he's gone."

"Are you religious?" Tom asked.

"Me?" Alvin looked at him in surprise. "Oh, I don't know. Not very, I guess."

"You ever go fishing?"

"Fishing?" Alvin was startled again. "Well, sure. Not lately. Why?"

Tom shrugged, suddenly self-conscious.

"Do you like to fish, Tom?"

"I've never been to Earth."

Alvin watched him for a moment, suddenly realizing what all this meant. "Where was your dad going to take you?"

"The Ozark Mountains." Tom spoke quietly, but looked up for Alvin's reaction.

"Oh, yes. The Ozarks. I've been canoeing there."

"That's what Dad wanted to do." Tom sat up eagerly in the recliner. "He said we could take a canoe all the way from the spring where a river started and float downstream on the current. And we could actually fish in the wild."

"You know, I could—" Alvin stopped abruptly. He had almost suggested taking Tom, but that wouldn't sound right. What Tom really wanted was his father's company, not the trip itself. Besides, Alvin couldn't handle the physical exertion anymore. "I could tell you a little about it," he finished quietly.

Tom shrugged again and slumped back into the recliner.

Alvin was still holding Tom's English paper. He smiled weakly, trying to force a joke. "In the old days we would have burned your paper so your father could have it. At one time we used to send things that way to people who had passed on. I guess no one believes in that now."

"What do you mean?" Tom asked. "No one believes in what?"

"Well, the old religion. The Chinese folk religion. When I was growing up in Chinatown—"

"You're from Chinatown?"

"Oh, yes. In Chicago. We had a shrine in the back of a little grocery store, not too far from Cermak. I was only a kid, of course."

"A shrine? Is that like an altar?"

"Well, sort of. We had all kinds of gods. No one was particular. We had Guan Yin, the goddess of mercy, and Guan Gong, the protector of travelers and the god of war. And Buddha, of course. Lots of others. People could go and pray and make sacrifices there. And anything you sacrificed to someone would go to that person's spirit in the other world."

"Do you believe that?" Tom asked carefully.

As Alvin looked at the young man, a lifetime of thoughts, opinions, and doubts about religion all churned in the back of his mind and faded away. He didn't know what he believed. As his own death neared, he wished more than ever that he did believe in something beyond life, but he didn't, not for sure. All he knew for certain was that at one time, as a child, he had believed what he had been taught, at least for a while.

"I think," Alvin said, "that it's a definite possibility."

"We're Episcopalians," said Tom.

"So was your father, then." That just came out; he didn't mean anything specific by it.

"Will you show me how to do it?" Tom asked timidly.

"Do what?"

"Make the sacrifice to my father."

Alvin looked at his face in the shadowed room. Tom was watching him anxiously, not pushing, but obviously eager. Alvin was surprised at his interest. Still, given the conversation, it was a perfectly reasonable request. The only problem was, Alvin wasn't sure he could remember how.

"Yes," said Alvin, with more confidence than he felt. "But now I am tired. We will talk more about it tomorrow."

Tom nodded and pushed himself out of the recliner. He nearly floated to his feet. "Good night, Grandpa."

A short time later, Alvin lay comfortably in the dark in his cubicle. He had many memories of the little shrine in Chinatown, but they were spotty—the sweet smell and drifting pale smoke of incense, his mother holding his younger sister in her arms, his father buying the artificial paper money in the front of the store and then burning it at the shrine. He fell asleep thinking of the glint of candlelight shining on the image of a carved wooden Guan Yin painted gold, sitting up high above him.

The next morning, after Tom was off to school and Ellen had left for work, Alvin sat alone with his tea in the kitchen. The aroma of the steam soothed him with its familiarity. For him, coming to live in space was something of an adventure, undoubtedly the last one in his life. It was ironic that his first challenge here was to remember scenes from a small urban storefront that had occurred over six decades ago. Last night he had been tired, but now he tried to organize his thoughts, and remember what he could.

Young Alvin had been an average kid, an okay student, something of a loner. He remembered standing with his family at the shrine. Sometimes people just made a donation and said a prayer, or left a written prayer on a stick or something. Other times, though, a full ceremony took place, where food and artificial paper money were sacrificed. The food was always the same: a fish, a chicken . . . what else? Some pork, he thought. Rice. The wine, of course. He shook his head in frustration. It had been so long ago.

When Tom came home that afternoon, he went right to his computer terminal without speaking to anyone. That suited Alvin, who was too embarrassed to tell him that he couldn't remember the sacrificial rites. He turned up the volume of the news and took Ellen aside. Casually, he asked if he had ever taken her to one of these ceremonies when she growing up. He couldn't even remember that much.

"I don't think so," said Ellen. "I don't remember going to anything like that."

"I guess I never went as an adult," said Alvin. "Most people in Chinatown were either Christians already or else they converted after a generation or so. Even when they didn't, if you left Chinatown, you didn't have one of those shrines to go to."

Ellen nodded, humoring him.

He remembered, then, that all his memories of the rites involved men and boys. The women had been present, however. Now that he thought about it, he also recalled that one branch of the family had refused to participate at all because they were Roman Catholic. They came, though, and watched while the other relatives performed the ceremony.

During dinner, Tom seemed to be in a good mood, but he didn't say anything about the rites. Alvin decided that Tom could be embarrassed by the request and might prefer not to let the whole family in on it. If so, it was too late to keep the matter from Ellen completely, but neither Alvin nor Ellen mentioned the subject during dinner, either.

After dinner, Alvin sat in the living room with Lisa. She showed him a couple of drawings she had made during art period earlier that day and demonstrated how to sketch cats and owls using only circles and triangles. Alvin tried it and got it wrong, laughing; she patiently showed him a second time. Meanwhile, Tom made himself scarce as long as Lisa was up.

Only moments after Ellen pried Lisa away to bed, Tom came out holding a small piece of paper.

"Uh, Grandpa?"

"Yes?" Alvin looked up, pleased at his grandson's polite tone.

"Does this look right?" Tom handed him the paper.

Alvin glanced at it and raised his eyebrows in surprise. "One whole chicken, clean; one whole fish, cleaned, often carp; a pork shoulder; rice; rice wine." He nodded, glancing over the list again. "Yes, this is right. Where did you get it?"

Tom grinned shyly with relief. "Well, I finally got it from the station library. I started with my computer terminal right after I got home, but I was looking in the school library. That didn't help any. Then I tried the station library, but I found all kinds of references on religion—too many. I had to check every one of them until I found this. I printed it out right away." His voice revealed a certain pride of accomplishment.

"That's what you've been doing all evening?"

"Yeah." He shrugged, still smiling.

"I'm impressed."

"But I never did find a reference that explained what you do with all this."

"I believe I can remember," said Alvin. "But can we get all we need here on the station? Up in space?"

"I guess so," said Tom. "Mom!"

Ellen came out of her bedroom. "Keep your voice down; Lisa's in bed. What is it?"

"Can we get all his stuff here on Hector?" He took the list from Alvin and gave it to her.

"Yes, but it's very expensive." She looked apologetically at Alvin. "Most of our meat and fish here is made from cloned tissue kept alive in nutrient tanks. We do ferment some wine up here, but I think the rice wine has to be imported. It could be very expensive."

"I'll reimburse you for all of it with my next pension check," said Alvin. "It's not much, but I can do that." He watched her face as she smiled slightly and gave the list back to Tom. She recognized the list, he was certain, especially after he had asked her about this subject earlier.

"Tell me when," said Ellen gently. "I'll go pick everything up for you." She went back to whatever she had been doing.

"We'll steam the rice and the fish," said Alvin thoughtfully to Tom. "We'll boil the chicken and the pork. For the wine, we need three little wine cups and a small wine pot."

"We have a Chinese tea set," said Tom.

"Perfect," said Alvin. "But we should ask your mother if we can borrow them. Now, then. What else?" He was asking himself.

Tom waited patiently.

"We need firecrackers and incense," said Alvin. "Can we get those here?"

"I can get incense in a novelty department," said Tom.

"But fireworks are illegal here."

"Even for religious reasons? Some cities down below make exceptions for religious purposes."

Tom shook his head. "Nothing like that has ever been available up here. Too dangerous. Security's real tight on space stations."

"I see." Alvin nodded, looking down at his hands. "Maybe some other kind of noisemaker. The idea is to scare away evil spirits." Privately, though, he didn't feel this ceremony would be right without firecrackers.

Alvin normally went to bed earlier than Tom, but tonight he made a point of staying up until his grandson was asleep. Then he approached Ellen as she made out her schedule for the next day in the dining area.

"Do you mind?" He sat down across from her.

She looked up, first surprised, then amused. "No. I don't mind."

"Are you sure? I mean, you're Episcopalian and all."

"I don't feel it's a contradiction, necessarily." She smiled, then cocked her head slightly. "But I overheard you tonight. Don't you need firecrackers to do it right?"

Alvin nodded.

"What are you going to do?"

He shrugged. "I don't know. Maybe nothing. But can you get me some paper?"

"Of course. I'll get some plain white paper for you tomorrow. But, um . . . ?"

"I need to draw some spirit money and cut it out into bills."

"Oh! Of course." She hesitated. "I don't want to

intrude, but can I help?"

"I think we'll be ready for that list of groceries tomorrow. That is, we might as well do this right away. The food has to be cooked, though, and I don't know how all your fancy space gadgets work—"

"We'll do it together," said Ellen, rising from her seat, nearly floating, to put an arm around him.

Late the next afternoon, Tom followed Carol Leggett, an old friend and classmate in several different subjects, down the darkened hallway. She stopped and palmed a doorlock, which hissed open. He glanced around nervously, but no one was in sight.

"Hurry up," she whispered, slipping inside.

He did, pushing the sidebar to close the door right behind him. She was a short, very pretty brunette with a rather stocky build. Her best class was chemistry, which had led to her position as lab assistant here. Her duties were to clean up used equipment and put everything away at the end of the school day, and she was trusted to come in and do so without teacher supervision.

"You better not be lying to me," said Carol, looking up at him with her blue eyes. "I wouldn't be doing this if it wasn't for your father and this religious thing."

"It's true," said Tom. "Besides, I'll do all the work."

"If anyone finds out I let you in, I'm the one who'll get in trouble," she said primly. "It won't matter who does what. Give me that list you showed me."

"Here."

"Well, let's see." She sat down at the computer terminal and called up the shelving number. "We have the first two ingredients, but . . ."

"But what?"

"What's charcoal?" She wrinkled her nose at him.

"Here, I'll show you. I already got some. They sell it with art supplies. I brought some cheap paper and string with me, too."

"I'll look later. I have to get to work cleaning up stuff. What else do you need?"

Tom looked at the instructions he had printed out from a reference file. It gave him the "recipe" for the chemical procedures he needed. "I just have to mix them up dry in certain measures. But then I have to wet the stuff with water and force it through a strainer and dry it again, to make grains."

"Here." She set down scales, small containers, and a beaker in front of him. Then she started her own duties.

Tom looked at the equipment in front of him, then at his list. He had never done well in chemistry, mostly because he got confused easily. "All right, let's see. First I have to weigh this little container, right?"

Carol looked up from a counter, holding five used beakers in clustered fingers. "If you're expecting me to do that for you, forget it—"

"Nobody's asking you," he said hotly, refusing to look up. "I just have to concentrate, that's all." Carefully, he measured each substance and combined them. Then he stirred the mixture, breaking the clumps into an even powder.

By the time he had finished mixing in a certain

amount of water and stirring the contents again, Carol had brought him a sieve that fit over a tray. Without a word, she showed him how to force his mixture through the screen. The result was small grains of the combined substance.

"I'll put it in the dryer under low heat," she said quietly, picking it up.

Tom picked up some dirty equipment and started washing it.

By the time the dryer buzzed gently, they had finished Carol's cleaning duties. She brought the tray out and set it on a counter. Tom poked through the grains with a glass rod.

"Gunpowder," he said, with a trace of awe. "You think it really works?"

"We don't dare test it," said Carol. "Too noisy and it will leave smoke. Besides, you didn't make enough to waste. And we have to hurry. I'm usually out of here by now."

"All right." Tom laid out the stack of small paper rectangles and the narrow, soft string he had brought. He started rolling the string in the powder, then found that rubbing it in worked better.

"Oh, no. This could take forever. All right, move over." Carol took the fuses as he cut them and laid them on the paper. She shook as much powder onto each paper as she could. Then, looking ahead, she fetched some paper paste.

As Tom rolled a thick layer of paper around each powdered fuse to make a tight bundle, she pasted the roll shut. They worked quietly, fumbling occasionally, but not seriously. As it turned out, Tom had enough supplies for twelve firecrackers.

Carol was just pasting the last one shut when the phone hummed. She jumped in surprise, then scooped all the firecrackers up and dumped them into Tom's hands. "Get out! Fast."

Tom didn't hesitate. He slipped out of the room as she answered the phone.

"Yes, Mr. Schwartz, I'm almost finished," she said breathlessly. "No, I'm alone. . . ."

The door hissed shut behind Tom as he walked briskly away, slipping his contraband into his pockets.

That night, Alvin stood by the back wall of the living room, looking at the arrangements he and Ellen had made. Most of the normal furniture had been pushed against the walls, out of the way. A large framed portrait photograph of Tom, Senior, had been hung on the front wall. Beneath it, a table had been set up with all the dishes Ellen had helped Alvin cook. Sticks of incense were stuck in a narrow vase, already burning to attract good spirits. In the front, Ellen's teapot held rice wine; three empty teacups were lined up in front of it, near the edge of the table.

Alvin felt a warm, tingling glow. It was right. He hadn't seen this sight for over half a century, but he recognized it. This was right.

Ellen was sitting off to one side, her arms around Lisa, who was standing in front of her. Lisa's hair had been tied into pigtails with red ribbon. She was looking around, wide-eyed, at everything. Tom stood on the other side of Alvin with a tight, self-conscious grin.

"The only thing missing is firecrackers," said Alvin. "But I guess we might as well start, so—"

"Here, Grandpop," said Tom, smirking with affected adolescent carelessness. His face reddened as he held out a handful of rather large, clumsily wrapped paper cylinders.

Alvin stared, then stifled a laugh of surprise as he accepted them. "Where . . . I thought you said those were illegal up here."

"They are," said Tom. "I made them in the chemistry lab."

"Uh . . ." Alvin turned to Ellen. "I don't know, that is, how serious it would be—"

"Go ahead," Ellen said firmly. She stood up and adjusted the ventilation system to work faster. "The noise may attract some attention, but I'll worry about that later."

Alvin looked down at the thick firecrackers. "When I was a kid, we lit these with matches. Or cigarette lighters."

"Open flames are severely discouraged," said Ellen. "I don't have anything like that, but I started the incense on a coil inside the stove. Come on, I'll show you."

Tom and Lisa followed Alvin after her.

Ellen turned a dial on the stove and then lifted a round cover from one burner, revealing the electrical insides. She pointed to a heavy wire. Alvin touched a fuse to it, and the fuse began to fizz and spark. He tossed the firecracker across the hard floor and lit another one. The first one banged loudly as he tossed down the third one. All together, nine of the twelve firecrackers went off; two more just fizzed and the last one did nothing.

"Go on," said Ellen, smiling. She nodded at the bits of paper and ash left behind. "The vent system will vacuum this up in a few minutes. If anyone comes knocking on the door, I'll answer it."

"All right." Alvin was grinning with satisfaction; he winked at Tom, who was fairly glowing. "Now, Tom, hand me the money."

Tom gave him the baking dish into which Ellen had put the artificial paper money Alvin had made. The drawings on the bills were very basic and sloppy, but it would do as a representation of cash to send to the spirit world.

Alvin lit the money the same way he had ignited the firecrackers and dropped the sheets into the baking dish. Then he returned the dish to the makeshift shrine. "Tom."

Tom stepped up to the front of the table.

Tom's report lay in a similar dish. Alvin took out one of the burning scraps of paper money and handed it to him. Tom took it, his mouth tense and serious. Carefully, he set his report on fire. Ellen held Lisa near the kitchen, watching it burn.

Alvin, strengthened by more bits of childhood memory and the role of old men in them, poured wine into the three empty cups. Tom stepped back from the table. Then, as the family eldest, Alvin went first, knowing that Tom would watch him carefully.

He clasped his hands together in front of him and bowed three times to his son-in-law's picture, each time raising his clasped hands over his head as he did so. The sweet scent of incense and the heavy smell of black powder, the fresh aroma of the food, the bouquet of the wine, and the long-forgotten gestures brought back not so much a clear memory as a wash of old, familiar comfort— a sense of stability and belonging.

After the third bow, he took one of the wine cups and poured the clear liquid onto the floor in a line from left to right in front of him. Then he repeated the ritual two more times, until all three wine cups were empty.

Alvin refilled the empty cups and stepped back, nodding to Tom.

Nervously, Tom came forward. As Alvin watched, young Tom repeated the bows, a little tentatively, but with a sober, serious expression. Then he glanced at Alvin as he reached for a wine cup.

At Alvin's nod, Tom completed the ritual by pouring the wine on the floor in front of him. He was more confident as he repeated the procedure twice more. Then, with a self-conscious grin of relief, he stepped back. The report was now merely a layer of ashes in the dish.

Alvin was reaching for the dish holding the chicken to carry it back to the kitchen when he saw Lisa watching him, her dark eyes as wide as they had ever been. He glanced up at Ellen and then motioned for Lisa to come forward. His own grandfather would not have approved, but Alvin was conducting this ceremony. Anyhow, his grandfather would never have understood *where* this was taking place, either—people living up in the sky?

Lisa came forward with slow steps, smiling shyly. Alvin refilled the empty cups and pointed to where she should stand. Carefully, she followed the examples of bowing she had just witnessed. Then she picked up the wine cup and dumped the contents on the floor, without drawing it in a line.

Grinning, Alvin whispered to her what to do with the next two cups. She nodded soberly and he stepped back. This time she completed the ceremony exactly right.

Alvin turned to see if Ellen wanted to participate, but she was standing with open arms as Lisa, now grinning broadly, ran back to her. In the same moment, Tom came forward and suddenly threw his arms around Alvin. Surprised, Alvin embraced him. Then Ellen, teary-eyed, and Lisa, her pigtails bouncing, came hurrying up to join in.

Alvin lived on Star Hector for about another year. He never quite got used to living in partial gravity, though it prolonged his life. The controls of many of the appliances, modified for life in space, remained a mystery to him, though he remained amused by the zero-gravity wok. Still, after conducting the sacrificial ceremony that day, he always felt that he was a part of this family.

It was not that Lisa sat in his lap any more often, or that Ellen was any more solicitous of his health than before. Afterward, though, the kids always showed him their schoolwork and their games. Further, without any prompting from him, they never again called him

"Grandpa," "Grandpop," or any other casual nickname. They called him "Grandfather."

Alvin liked that. He thought sometimes of the old men in Chicago, whose own grandfathers and great-grandfathers had brought these ceremonies and rituals with them across the Pacific from one continent to another. He liked thinking that he was another link in the same chain, having brought—with the help of Tom and his computer and his chemistry lab—the same rituals across an even greater gulf to yet another world. Most of all, he liked thinking that he had invited young Tom to be the next link.

Young Tom didn't experience any miraculous change of personality, of course. He remained a fair, but rather bored, student. However, he did develop a greater interest in chemistry. Any time he discussed it with Alvin, they always spoke as if they shared some special secret.

When Alvin died in his sleep of heart failure, Tom prevailed on Carol for one more favor in the chemistry lab. This time, the work went faster and more efficiently. He did all the chemistry himself, without any need for her help.

In the privacy of the family apartment, Tom set up the shrine with his mother's preparations. He laid it beneath two photos on the wall. One was of his father, Tom Leong, Senior, and the other was of his maternal grandfather, Alvin Kwok.

Young Tom was the one who lit the incense, burned the spirit money, poured the wine, and of course set off the firecrackers.

AFTERWORD

The material for this anthology was developed during the time I taught creative writing in Asian American Studies at the University of California, at Berkeley and at Santa Barbara. I learned far more from my students than they learned from me.

In the past, children's writers (and this unfortunately includes some early Asian American writers) have portrayed Asian Americans in the crudest and clumsiest terms. Sometimes their fictional Asian Americans were unassimilated aliens who would always remain apart. Or more frequently these writers described the Asians as wanting to be as American as they could be. Anything American was automatically good. Anything Asian became bad, and a set of cultures more than four millennia old was depicted as being backward, superstitious, or downright dangerous.

Readers interested in learning about Asian American history will want to read Sucheng Chan's *Asian Americans, An Interpretive History*. Ron Takaki's *Strangers from Another Shore* is another possibility.

Elaine Kim's *Asian American Literature* provides a useful survey up to 1982. Her emphasis, however, is on adult books, and it stops before the recent explosion of titles for children.

In speaking to various groups across the country, I

have been asked for standards to use in evaluating stories about Asian American children. Elaine Kim presents some criteria in her book. Readers may also find it useful to adapt some of the yardsticks that Rudine Sims Bishop applies to the portrayal of people of color in *Shadow and Substance*; children's writers have unfortunately made similar mistakes in depicting both people of color and Asian Americans. Of similar use are Opal Moore and Donnarae McCann's examination of the portrayals of Latino and Native Americans in children's books.

The writers in this anthology have each shown a different face of Asian America, a face that bears the stamp not only of a common humanity but also of its own uniqueness. Like Asian America, they have the supple strength of dragons.

RECOMMENDED
BIBLIOGRAPHY

Rudine Sims Bishop (writing under the name Rudine Sims), *Shadow and Substance* (Urbana, Ill.: NCTE, 1982).

Sucheng Chan, *Asian America, An Interpretive History* (Boston: Twayne Publishers, 1991).

Elain H. Kim, *Asian American Literature* (Philadelphia: Temple University Press, 1982).

Opal Moore and Donnarae MacCann, "The Ignoble Savage: Amerind Images in the Mainstream Mind," in *Children's Literature Association Quarterly*, Vol. 12, No. 1 (Spring 1987).

———. "Paternalism and Assimilation in Books About Hispanics," in *Children's Literature Association Quarterly*: Part One in Vol. 12, No. 2 (Summer 1987), Part Two in Vol. 12, No. 3 (Fall 1987).